Border Arts:
Beyond The
Barriers

Cover art, design, and editing
by Gabriel H. Sanchez
Visit: theravingpress.com

ISBN: 978-0-9989965-9-2

The Raving Press, 2022
Mission, Texas

PREFACE

The following are works of art in images, poetry, and prose by writers, poets, photographers, and visual artists living in (or creating works about) the U.S.-Mexico border states. Their order of appearance in the Contents page, the body, and the Contributor Bios section is at random. No one person, or work of art, whether appearing first or last is less or more than the others. We are transcending the barriers of race, color, sex, creed, and nationality. The purpose of this book and future efforts is to create a strong sense of unity through our shared identity and art. These are the creators painting the face of the border and telling the stories that shape its reality. These are the works of the artists creating the border in their image.

CONTENTS

FOREWORD
by Kathleen Bunyan Carlson

A political border runs along the southern United States. It separates California, Arizona, New Mexico, and Texas from Mexico. It is a fake border. It cannot be seen from Space. This border does not prevent the people who live along that imaginary line from sharing the treasures of their common heritage and experience.

This anthology is the dynamic expression of that sharing. The artists in this collection use words. Others use paint and clay, music and glass, song and performance, food and textiles. The Arts are among the strongest forces shaping the people and the reality of life in this area.

The people here share out of and share in the cultures and history of the Originals, the Spanish, the Mixed, the Anglos and the Africans. This combination makes their expression distinctive and colorful. There is none like it in the rest of the world. The people are warm yet reserved, welcoming yet careful, guileless yet wise. Their strength comes from their grip on the earth. Their vision springs from conquering and being conquered.

Here are poems, prose, short stories and photos. They depict immigration, love, crime, history, family, strangers and more of life along the border.

Step over the line, dear reader.

I dare you.

MUJER, SOMOS RÍOS
by Julieta Corpus

Mujer, somos ríos
Sólo en sueños puedo ver
Esos ríos que los Mixtecos dicen
Llevamos por dentro las mujeres.
Mis ríos a veces son verdes
Como las hojitas de yerbabuena
Que sembraba mi abuela Lola
En botecitos de latón.
Otras veces son azules como el
Cielo impasible sobre los cerros
Del viejo pueblo donde crecí.
En sueños, he visto ríos turbulentos
Vomitando mis miedos cuando la vida
Me estruja el alma.
Todos ellos son ríos que las mujeres
Llevamos dentro.
Y cuando se desbordan, sus aguas
Salen de nosotras como llanto, sudor,
Orina, saliva, y sangre.
Escucha, mujer: Somos llanto.
Escucha, mujer: Somos sudor.
Escucha, mujer: Somos orina.
Escucha, mujer: Somos saliva.
Escucha, mujer: Somos sangre.
Mujer, somos ríos.

PIEDRA COMÚN
by Julieta Corpus

Soy piedra en el desierto
Siguiendote los pasos;
Sé que ibas al encuentro
De una vida mejor.
Quisiera que al mirarme
Acudiera a tu mente
Un tal Chente Fernandez,
Y su bella canción:
Una piedra en el camino
Me enseno que mi destino
Era rodar y rodar. No tengo
Trono ni reina, ni nadie quien
Me comprenda, pero sigo
Siendo el rey!
Quisiera que a tu mente
Le fueran brotando alas,
Transportandote al pueblo
Testigo de tu andar.
Allí donde tu madre
Descansa de sus males,
Y tu viejo del alma
Siempre te esperará.
Ninguna de tus gentes

Quiso que te marcharas:
"Mejor aquí te quedas que
Allá está mal la cosa.
Tus primos y amistades
No volvieron jamás.
Pero no hiciste caso ni
A ellos ni a tu esposa,
Viste hambre en su mirada
Y en la de tus chamacos,
"Les juro que regreso,
Nomás junte dinero.

Yo me cuido solito;
Me encargo a Dios del cielo".
Maldita la avaricia
Que tiraniza al hombre;
La misma que hoy te tiene
Sangrando y casi muerto.
Maldito sea el coyote.
Maldita la miseria.
Malditos sean los muros.
Malditos los gobiernos.
Soy el testigo mudo;
Soy piedra del desierto.

BORDERS, ECHOES WITHIN
by Rosalva Ruiz

As I was waiting at the international border
a thunder was heard.
A flock of birds flew from below.
It was not just a blast and silence,
but an echo that went for miles in violence.
And you might ask,
how would you know?
It was the movement of the birds,
frantically escaping away from what I saw.

Soon after, like a stampede,
a group of teenagers were running away
towards Mexico's side of the bridge.
Some were white,
others were black,
and a few were brunettes,
but the Asian one got my attention.
He came walking with no perturbation.

That got me thinking…
How deep are our borders?
Some borders are for intruders, others for robbers,
there are also for the undocumented and the unwanted.
Then again, those are but physical borders.

What about our internal borders?
They seem to have been constructed since our childhood.
Some were born from our parents' views over the years,
yet others were born from our very own fears.

People seemed to be walking between walls.
Some are much more equipped than most of us,
I guess it's because of their jobs.
Some others are just for show,
maybe because of their internal disputes

over their own glow.
And let's not forget the glasslike ones,
They show themselves as they are;
However, you can't even leave a speck,
Or else they'll wipe it on the spot…

Others are spotless, but internal screams will echo within.
I sometimes wonder, which is my border?
Have you?

Oh! Finally!
After the shooting and the running
The agents finally opened the border again.
Been waiting for more than thirty minutes…
My mind has also slipped away through those hurdles.
Better have my papers ready
and not make a mistake.
Should I go through the "All Documents,"
Or the ready lane?

Whichever it is, got nothing to hide.
I just came to see my family
and replenish my heart.
Now I'm going back to my house,
to my life, and yes,
probably also to those walls…

Once again,
screams will echo within my borders.
Once again,
I become the observer
with no movement at all…

CAMINANTE AL
ANDAR
by Rosalva Ruiz
(SuperNova)

Caminante al andar,
que te la juegas al azar,
para a tus hijos un mejor
futuro
poderles dar.

Caminante al andar,
entre montes, montañas
y ríos haz de pasar
para a la tierra prometida,
poder llegar.

Caminante al andar,
tu vida de nómada
empezaras.
Política, fronteras y
orgullo dejas atrás.
Por pueblos, ciudades y
países has de pasar.

Caminante al andar,
tu futuro empiezas a
forjar.
Mojado, indocumentado,

llanta negra
te han de llamar
mas con tus fuerzas
internas
tus metas haz de lograr.

Caminante al andar,
tu tierra dejas atrás.
Con nuevos idiomas,
nuevos miedos,
nuevas destrezas y nuevas
culturas te haz de topar.
Más aun así, tu sueño no
desistirá.

Caminante al andar,
aunque tu orgullo dejas
atrás,
de ti emana un ego difícil
de sobrepasar
Y eso te da fuerzas para
llegar.

Caminante al andar,
tu casa encontrarás.
Tu sacrificio, tu esfuerzo,
tus pesares y anhelos
por fin fruto te darán.

MY ROLE IN LA FRONTERA
by SuperNova [Rosalva Ruiz]

A patriot of the zone.
The sole bearer of my soul.
The only prisoner of my shortcomings.
A refugee of a painful past
across the border.
Longing to see my roots,
yet in constant battle
to uphold my foot.
The whisperer of my dreams
and also, the anchor of my wings.

The chained voice of my past
Por el que dirán.
Not that I care,
but have to keep
a show 'cause I care for her.
Even if the consequences
hurt my soul.

I'm also the keeper
of three little souls.
Without knowing,
I have become
a voice for past souls
and their surroundings.
Also, the observer
Of current development
Surrounding our city.

Although,
I'm just another number to the government,
I'm one of the voices of The Valley.
I bring riches to the soil
and cultivate their soul
Hopefully in the future,
I get to admire the fruits
these little seeds bear.

'Dirty Hands' by Amanda Lee Calderon'

'Locked Away' by Amanda Lee Calderon

'These Walls' by Amanda Lee Calderon

THROUGH THE BORDER FENCE
by Yolanda Chávez Leyva

"Through the Border Fence" is a photographic project that asks the questions: What can we learn about border life by looking through a fence instead of simply allowing it to divide us from our neighbors? What can we see through a fence intended to separate us and obscure our view?

Grounded in El Paso, Texas/ Ciudad Juárez, Chihuahua, the photographs are a call to examine life on the Mexican side of the border through the uniquely U.S. experience of looking through the border fence. It is an invitation to reflect on our relationship with the border and with our neighboring community. It is an encouragement to connect with humanity despite the presence of a two-story tall, rust-colored barrier.

In only six minutes, I can drive from my campus, park, and walk up to the border fence facing Ciudad Juárez. It is a quick and safe trip to the fence. For migrants moving from the south to the north, there is no safety in their journey to the fence. By the time they arrive at the fence, many will have traveled thousands of miles on foot and by bus. To reach the fence, they must swim across the Rio Grande/ Rio Bravo and then the American Canal, both seemingly safe yet filled with surprisingly strong undercurrents. Each May, Juárez organizations pass out flyers urging migrants not to try to swim across the river because of this danger. Each year there are drowning deaths.

The fence literally and symbolically distorts our view of Ciudad Juárez. The tight weave of the fence makes it impossible to view the other side clearly. As a child driving in the back seat of my parents' car, I could look out the window and see the houses, the river, the families picnicking on its banks. Now, I drive the same roads with a two-story fence obscuring the other side, rising menacingly beside me.

The presence of the fence reinforces the idea that we are on *this* side. With a fence, there is always a *here* and a *there, this side* and *that side, us* and *them*. On a physical level, the

10

U.S.-constructed fence is supposed to keep out migrants although countless desperate migrants try to climb over the fence each year. Hundreds are injured or die trying to climb over it. They become statistics or flashes of news. The fence hides their humanity and becomes a site of danger and death.

This project calls on us to look deeply through the fence where fragments of day-to-day life are visible laundry hanging to dry on a porch, the brightly colored homes that are part of a 2017 mural project, the solitary boredom of a Border Patrol officer, or the "auxilio" ("help") sign posted on this side, evidence that the fence doesn't always work. Even without the presence of people, the images are filled with life.

by Yolanda Chávez Leyva

CUANDO SEA POSIBLE
by Luke Van Garza

Chonita awoke, as she always did, alone. A faint sliver of light coming from underneath the bathroom door told her Chemo was shaving. She heard the razor scrape against his whiskers, followed by a gentle splashing as he plunged the blade into the water to rinse it off. Comforted by the sounds, she curled up into a ball. Es una cosa de hombres--a ritual, simple, yet distinctly masculine. She wondered if he would be similarly aroused by the sight of her shaving her legs. As if he had the luxury of time to watch her. Saddened by this last thought, she dressed quietly, made the bed, and went to the kitchen.

In the dark she located the box of matches by pure instinct. She struck a match and held it to the invisible gas flow of the stove. The blue flame crackled for an instant, violated by a small incursion of unpure, sulfuric smelling gas, then an accompanying scent of burnt protein. Chonita leaned in for a closer look. Underneath the burner lay a freshly torched cockroach. The match still lit; she waved it across the wall like an explorer's torch in the Parisian catacombs. More roaches scattered to darker recesses of the room. Satisfied, she opened the oven door, slid out the cast iron comal and placed it over the flame.

Soon she was slapping the masa between her hands in a rhythmic patty-cake fashion. This was her ritual, the culmination of mixed flour and water, cupped into a ball, then smoothed flat by the rolling pin. She went through the process three times for each tortilla before laying them on the comal, en el nombre del Padre, del Hijo, del Espiritu Santo.

The coffee can was nearly empty. She didn't have the heart to tell Chemo this, because she knew he wouldn't be paid for another week. Using a paper towel, she strained the remnants of old grain from the blue metal pot and added a pinch of new stuff to the mixture.

Chemo emerged from the bathroom, toweling his face. His day had not yet begun, but already the heat from the shaving water had produced damp crescents at the underarms of his white muscle tee. This too aroused her, so she forced herself to look away and tend to the tortillas.

13

She fetched a salvaged piece of aluminum foil from a kitchen drawer and began piling the tortillas onto it. Behind her she detected the familiar sound of Chemo fumbling through the kitchen cabinet for his lunchbox, which he always kept on the highest shelf. She contemplated why he put it way up there…probably to keep it out of the kids' reach. He certainly didn't like them messing with his things, and this, perhaps, was the nicest thing he owned. It was her gift to him from last Christmas, a smooth black plastic box that came with its own thermos.

Chemo extracted the pot from the flame and gingerly poured the liquid into his thermos. Chonita turned slowly to face him, all the while continuing to flip tortillas off the hot comal with her bare fingertips. Their eyes locked for a second.

Chemo became unnerved and shifted his glance down to the comal. "You're cooking them too long," he said. "I don't like them tostaditas."

He spoke with authority, but she did not shrink back or tremble because there was no hint of violence in his tone. The words arrived softly, so as not to wake the kids, matter-of factly. She knew his preferences, and in esta manera he came as close as she knew he ever would to a daily affirmation of his love for her.

Chemo tucked the foil-encased tortillas into his lunch box. He made for the door, feigning hurriedness, but his step slowed just enough to let her words catch up.

When will I see you again? she wanted to say, all the while picturing a long embrace, his pleated khakis unbuckled, his body sliding onto hers, not even bothering to unfold the patchwork quilt beneath them. But she knew he would never have time for such things, so she settled for, "When should I expect you?" "About 8:30 en la noche," he mumbled, and left.

REMEMBER ME
by Luke Van Garza

He was always good at keeping promises, Luz thought.

He never broke a single one.

Luz nudged the old cane rocker with his damp work boot, setting the chair into a gentle motion. Sudden dizziness rocked his head, thoughts emptying into an awakening stream, flooding, until he could sense the backwaters lapping against the edge of his braincase, threatening to spill over.

"Who's talking to me?" he spat out. "God?"

He tried to swim against it, tried to fill his mind with thoughts of a hard day's work, couple of beers at the lounge, saving up enough to get Mamá a microwave, finally taking his G.E.D....but the one voice stuck out amongst the horde of others, stuck out like a sore thumb until it grew swollen and purple and festered and quickly rotted into a bare white essence.

"Mi'jito, I'm coming back to you," the weak raspy voice, lightly accented, floated through him. It had serenaded Luz with an old-fashioned corrido, a ballad of Gregorio Cortes...and a touch of Bacardi on the breath. Maybe once too often, Mamá would've said.

"Maybe not enough," Luz whispered to himself.

"I'm coming back to you," the voice croaked on. "I won't be gone for long, my child. En diez años, mi'jito. Count them."

And Luz had clutched the threaded blue veins in his grandfather's hand. He'd been waiting for the key words.

"That's a promise."

Papá Juan had breathed his last.

It was raining today, just as it had back then. Does God give everyone a rainy day when they die? The swirl of thoughts finally slowed, and he began picking off the strays like ducks at a tin pan alley, each bobbing down one by one.

It was my birthday, the day he died. My birthday...and his. Luz sent that one smack into the water. Home. Here. This place, this...chair. The rocking chair.

He didn't die in the hospital, with all those I.V.s pumping crap up his veins and tubes in his nose. He had died here, en esta casa, este cuarto, esta... mecedora. The rocking chair. Like he had wanted.

"Recuerdate."

Luz brought the rocker to a full stop and concentrated. But nothing came to him. A waste. What a waste. How can I explain this to Mamá? I've stayed away from work for a whole day, all for some crazy dead man's promise. I'll be out of a job at the icing docks. We'll have no money and then she'll kill me.

"Quieres un sartenaso?" he could hear his mother screaming. "¿Que 'stas haciendo, tonto?"

Tonto. He was crazy, to be staying home on a day like this. Even if it was his birthday...and Papá Juan's.

"Screw this," he said aloud, and made for the door.

Hair on the back of his head prickled. Luz felt a sharp static discharge knock on his skull. He lunged

16

at the doorknob, but his hand fell short. A low buzzing echoed inside his fist. Luz opened his hand, gaping at his palm. "Colmena!"

The bee planted its sting squarely in the middle. "Chingau!"

Luz smashed the little terror into a dark smudge and wiped it off on the wall next to the light switch.

The door slammed shut abruptly beside him. "Mouth like a sewer!"

The dull 40-watt bulb above flamed rapidly into stage light blindness. Luz's shadow fell flat across the door.

Another one joined it, rising straight up behind him. Fear gushed out of him, liquid warmth down his leg.

"Now, now...you don't have to be doing **that**."

Luz struggled, mouthed the word until it came into fruition. It had been ten years since he had last used it.

"¿'Buelo?"

"Turn around, mi'jito, so I can see you."

He quarter-turned, catching light flares out the corner of his eye. The room rotated to meet him, momentum swinging him like a merry-go-ound. Circles of brightness burned into his retinas. Spreading the fingers of his hand, he filtered the glare and spotted the maroon folds of a bathrobe, but no one inside it.

"I can't see you," Luz said finally.

"Of course not. I don't exist in the flesh anymore, what's the matter with you?"

It was the sharp sting, something Mamá had inherited, something Luz hated in her. But to hear it again, from Papá Juan...

"Remember me," the voice continued. "Only then can you see. Recuerdate."

Luz tried again, dammed the river of fear and ignorance and anger by moments, until the figure of Papá Juan bloomed softly into his vision like the image on an old picture tube. There was a trace of ruddiness to his high Indian cheekbones. Wrinkles smoothed away to reveal crisp olive skin. His frame stood thin, angular, and tall, commanding a renewed sense of respect. The grandfather raised one hand, pressed a lip-moistened cigarette to his mouth.

"I can smoke as many of these as I want," Papá Juan chuckled. "¡Que barbara!"

"¿'Buelo?" Luz said. "What are you doing here?"

"Don't pretend you don't remember. ¿Te prometi, reda? I always keep my promises." Papá Juan motioned to an old rolltop desk nestled beside the bedroom window. "Top drawer on the right. Open it."

Luz obeyed.

"Feel around the top of the inside for a key. You got it? Okay, take it down to First National. Ask for Drawer 72." Papá Juan's tabby grey pupils mirrored Luz's wide-eyed response. "You know what it's for." Luz started to say something, then simply nodded. "What about Mamá?"

Papá Juan eased into the rocking chair. "She can always ask for her old job at the courthouse. I didn't raise any of my kids to be flojos, you know. Or idiots." He puffed softly on his cigarette. "'You taken your G.E.D.?" "No." Luz stamped one boot uncomfortably.

"Well, I don't have time for stories." The grandfather sighed, blinked his eyes heavily, and began to fade.

Luz grew frantic. "Wait, 'buelo!"

"En diez años, mi'jito," the man said, smiling. And then he was gone. The light dimmed; the thoughts receded. Luz remained for a moment, nursing a residual pain in the palm of his hand. He knew he would not go back to the icing docks that day, or the day after. He knew Mamá would probably scream at him for enrolling at the community college, and demand to know where he got the money and why he wasn't spending it on her. He knew these things, but most of all he knew the briefness of visits. Luz left the room, knowing full well he would return there in another decade, but for now there was no time to waste.

THE BRIDGE
by AE Reiff

The images flow upward from down below too. The tribal folk
along the river give up visions and sound. Home and Rome
become Holmes. Songs in this state of mind wear chartreuse
clothes with yellow scarves and dandy hats that impersonate
the night jars. Of fireflies. The ones below impersonate the
ones above on a two way up and down. The up and down are
one, the down up, the up down one. Projections of poems sail
from the bridge, which is not over or under either, but around
and through. Water birds inhabit winged trees there where high
herons dive. On the hill shoulder, pears and parables of
sunlight descend to a rookery where Democracy makes love in
her Sunkist hair on the alabaster plain of the moon. Winds turn
the mother of pearl to blue. There are no lands or sun or stars.
The crowd is singing of itself—House and Mouth, but neither
exist in that way except as radiant abyss. Just the opposite of
pure vacancy

Once this was called empirical thought, well designed, but
don't take my word for it, see for yourself. The boots of the
kings lay in contempt upon the tomes of the books like necks,
whose heads have been left below in the trees. Book heads,
nicely bound in leather, lay on the ground like Egyptian
mummies, at nice 7-degree angles too. In a party game two
players lift their arms and others pass beneath. Holding the
shoulders of the one before they hurry lest they be caught. The
descending arms of the game are a good place to start, but the
game ends in a tug of war. The bridge becomes a tug where
neither win. The bridge connects both worlds.

Flying like butterflies in fall about the heads and necks of the
Bridge travelers, swallows of different colors dart in and out.
Hawks and chickens, ducks, white and red orange parrots thick
as leaves in a wind. These are thoughts. We call these bridges

because those who cruise the lobbies of river mouths do. We should call them divine gates, and the beautiful, puffed birds, powerful, corrupt, grotesque, are everything that could be said of bobbling on one foot.

The bridges suspend from even greater reconstituted towers which fit the quantum structo, both and neither. We merely observe the algorithms, concurrent with our sympathy that runs in waves. In the case of vulgar idiots who profane this wilderness with every breath, the proof for this quantum info is to sell it to the masses with that analogy of plus, minus, either both or maybe neither. In quantum landscape either/or every hill will valley, and every valley hill, and both maybe together invent a numbering beyond 100 where you stop.

There is a double strand of layers on whose upper deck long legged thrones sit in rows whose feet hang down. Gyres of immortal turpitudes of their feet hang down and glow. Feet and head connect as an ampersand. Under their seats endless hedgerow volumes of commentary and journal in every language stretch from one end of the bridge to the other. This is the reality that the thrones as rulers are creating for their kings on the lower deck, who indulge this ferment by projecting it in the violent passion of riddles in the dreams of those below, the moon chained villages that live on the river and the ground. Suspended from the deck so they could be seen by the villages on the ground, dingle stars in radium pyres flash beside the thrones like fireflies in nightjars. These were the stars that lit the wishes always rising. They could as easily have been plum trees that grew crooked over the rivers overhung with ripe fruit to feed the gulls that circled in and out like wheels in wheels out of the eyes.
So far, the bridge has kept from falling. Some say it's a bridge of iron and steel to cross but it's a bridge to build the world. In all its inimical stand. Our Brupper entrained his loose clothing with nano bats that charged when he walked, harvesting from eyelids and venous return, arterial pulse, and footsteps. This enabled the veritable to walk. It needed electric don't you see. To participate, suffer, sacrifice, feel pain with those named. The Colonist's step over this bespelled floor was All in One. It came on as swift as a car slam as you walk or your legs

21

flow to the pavement of themselves. There, one and all, at midnight with false papers, we are commanded to walk.

Who will you think he is and how will you know? But how could he have a name, he is one who came the way all of us might think we have, special to ourselves without doubt, trumpets of fantasy mind, until reason kicks it out. How does anybody escape? In public character, seeming humble and empathic, to be as interested as much as I am in this one with no name, this every man came down from the sun on ice waves and hydrogen fire of forgetful joy to the world so wrapped up in his coming one forgets the exit. Then the brain waves change. Oh, you didn't know it is coming, takes about seven decades later to get the news, lust, peace, hope, death.

So, we don't have a name for him, never did even if we have been writing about him all his life, a little obtuse in his pretending, but with the ability to dance, no need to think him different from any other despite the scientific studies that justify his steps. He's a dancer making onion skins to cover up the nothing new, so he has no name when all the coverings are taken away, although we insist on his dignity.
Surface memory what I said to you, just now forgotten, and the dozens of layers below it, all down to base memory of the horrors done us by circumstance that permeates through the other layers up, never forgotten but replayed, these things I think and don't, as a kind of decoder's manual, believe nothing and everything according to the truth. Unacceptable premises proving and disproving the mythologies of the world. The world is false, I burn the dross, nothing is revealed.

THE GREATEST LITERARY CRITIC I HAVE EVER HAD
by Victor M. Parlatto

Bella,
I had just gotten home from my cashier job
and I was exhausted and not nearly as drunk
as other days.

my mom was
in the front yard, holding two or four pieces of paper
to her chest
and looking at me.

"your father read your poetry," she said.

"which ones?"

"all of them. even the one about the
bullfighter," she said.
she looked beaten
and eyes swollen
from crying.

I had a cigarette in my hand,
lit and near its end;
I tossed it at the wet grass,
entered my father's home,
and saw him at the kitchen table,
still reading those poems and even some of the ones
I had under my bed in a brown box labelled "POSSIBLE
BOOK/CHANGE NAME".

"I read them," he said, tired ugly eyes picking my
reaction piece by piece.

"yeah. mom told me.
what do you think?"

"I hate them,
but I did enjoy the bullfighter.
it's about me, isn't it?"

"it could be," I told him.

"I think it is," he said.

he didn't say anything after that.
my mother came in
and we ate dinner, my poems stuffed back
in their boxes
under the kitchen table,
and I knew my father had accepted his Hispanic
disappointment in all of it:

to have a son that carries his name and says nothing to him;
a wife that says too much and who accepts her role like an old
dress, like old worn out shoes;
and a first-born son that chose to write poetry for a living—

LOVE IS A CAT ON THE BOUGH
by Victor M. Parlatto

Bella,
after a breakup, I rarely find myself
thinking about the loss I took in having
such great legs, such great ass, such great breast
walk across my room, pick up clothes and move out almost
as quickly as they came in.

but sometimes—
like tonight—
as I sit on this queen size bed
with two canker sores in the roof of my mouth,
overworked and underpaid, and un-fucked,
I do catch myself missing the strange amenities of a woman:

like a home cooked meal;
like a warm body to rest against;
like another person to
pit against during times of difficulty;
like finding one of their socks under a bed,
an earring inside the sheets, a scrunchie in the dirty basket;
like a morning fuck, an afternoon fuck, an evening fuck, hell,
even
just a fuck just to fuck; a fuck
when times are tough; a fuck when
times are good; a fuck when times are sad;
a fuck when times are mad;

or
like getting in a shower

and finding their cunt hair
circled around the shower drain;

or having someone to settle your bones after
death...

even now, I watch out my apartment window,
just a little after 10 PM, and
a white cat leaps up the tree in front of me.

it sits on the bough and watches me through the open blinds.
it does not move. it does not blink.

and then it is gone.

DIFFICULT LOVERS
by Victor M. Parlatto

(REDACTED),
you said I was difficult to love,
as you wrote inkless poems
on my back and chest.

but I remember your birthday;
I remember your eyes the moment
you realized you fell in love,
hiding your vulnerability in the shadows of
my one-bedroom apartment;

I remember your church, my silence,
your smile from person to person
as I cowered in the back of every conversation;

I remember your hands like paint brushes
across my canvas flesh, your breath
against mine, your sounds rare and raw
as they fought to escape my
prison;

and I remember how you
left me:
a lengthy Facebook message
at 10 PM, Monday.

you believe I have a difficult heart
when I think
I'm just a difficult person.

you believe I'm hiding in my poems

27

while I'm just trying to exist, my lips
bound shut by the strings of my heart,
my poems becoming my only artistic expression.

you believe I'm afraid of change, but I'm
only changing what I believe is possible,
ego boasting the novel of my life,
written by the smartest idiot alive.

and you believe I'm traveling through
the haze of my memories, grey and blue,
while I'm
just trying not to forget
your birthday.

DESAFIO
by Don E. Peavy Sr.
(To Bianca)

Out of the glistening sands of Santander, Spain;
Meandering through the mountainous morass that is Mexico;
Breaking across the border of bright beginnings:
Frazzled, famished and found with child –
Like Hagar stumbling through the unpromised land:
Used, abused, and cast adrift;
Struggling for life for a dying child;
Hoping beyond hope that there is justice
Beyond the wiles of man and the hands of fate.
Up from despair by hands of mercy;
Learning the language of a new land;
Working overtime to repay the costs
Of a forlorn journey and delicate delivery.
From these things and more have you emerged

With grace, dignity, and light;
Proving once again the fire that inflamed
Prometheus and Sisyphus yet burns –
Even in the heart of a woman-child
Who is now a woman of unequaled beauty –
A rare jewel in the crown of heaven!

For each pain you suffered,
Each injustice you endured,
You responded with "quiet grace" and dignity –
Becoming what many aspire to be
But few ever become.
You cut the strings of the gods
That wreak havoc in human lives;
Who bestow upon humans free will
Then force them to surrender to that of the gods.
Now, your time has come.
The stars have aligned in your favor –
The lost of Juliet and her Romeo
Has become your gain.
Heaven smiles to see what you were
And what you have become.

You have come up from dying in the dust
To shining as a star;
Excelling as a mother;
Reincarnating Florence Nightingale.

In your defiance of culture, clan, and cultus,
You have given hope that humans
Might rise above chance, circumstance, and condition
To a wondrous height
Beyond the Roché limit of the gods
Against which Icarus collided
And crashed to earth to rise no more.

Truly you are a rare jewel in the crown of heaven –
I kneel before your holy face
And kiss your tender hand
Unmarred by life's cruel work.
On bended knee am I enlightened
to the reality that heaven is on earth.

1. "EL PASO OLDEN
DAYS MEXICAN"
HAIKU
by Gerard Sarnat

8000 laying
hens on our farm crossed
Juarez
border like the street.

2. "IF I ONLY KNEW
THEN WHAT I KNOW
NOW"
by Gerard Sarnat

Testosteroned twenties -

pay thugs to make sure
guns

and knives are left outside

the clinic's board room
door,

employ supposed ally

Ayo's Bonanno* slugs

to sweep the telephones

for bugs - I am run off

the road by ethnic groups

who moo, "Whitey's Heb
gang

is stealing our cash cow."

*Bonanno headed an East
Coast mafia family

31

3. "HOW BONANNO SLIMED FLEAS LIKE ME"
by Gerard Sarnat

You never talk in a club,
you never talk in a car,
you never talk on a cell,
you never talk on a phone,
you never talk in your house;
only do roving walk-talks.

BALLAD OF THE CHECKERBOARD
by Ana M. Fores Tamayo

A white man wearing judges' robes
was standing in the midst of all that brown,
next to some rabble rousers, all incensed.
These firebrands came to speak up for the brown Garcia
family, although they did not know the murdered man.
These instigators were the only other whites,
as far as I could tell,
although I thought they were a bit inane,
these open carry types.

They caused a real ruckus.

These fatuous fools started chanting
while another white man dressed in uniform
standing upright, by the podium, told them to please
consider shutting up. The browns looked on,
shamed-faced. But this poor white trash bellowed they would
never quiet down. Never give their floor to freedom without
guns.

The white man judged again,
told them to suppress their thoughts or go away,
yet seeming to confuse his words,
he roared: go back to your own country,
where it is that you belong.

Was he speaking to the browns or to the whites?
.
Lucky it was City Hall I guess,
and folks were calmer overall
than any other place where riots take a turn...
The whites resumed to yell and scream:
but we are white, we are supreme,
we do belong here:
what of you?

© City Hall by Ana M. Fores Tamayo

The browns looked onward,
shunning the clashing clique,
lamenting no one came to mourn
their son their brother their lover friend.
This refuse only came to make a point of their big guns,
using poor folks' murders to lay some blame.
But still, they could not take away the grief unfolding
of that sorrowful brown hued girl,
her four young children grasping at her skirts,
crying for their own lost daddy,
their loved and lost best friend.
Oh my.

FISHING IN THE GREEN
by Ana M. Fores Tamayo

Two bleached blond heads standing by
the midst of green-manicured lawns
gently sloping the golf balls
peeking near a hole-in-one.

Erect and standing tall, boy and girl
look over the vast verdant sea
searching for blue, a blue dot in that endless jade
where they can dip their poles into:
long, thin, expert poles
with string ready at the bite to get that fish…
but in the green?

Close by the boy's shiny steel-blue truck
pridefully shining in the sun stands still,
holding all that fishing gear,
the buckets to keep the fish once they've bitten their bait,
the bait to tantalize the fish…
but wait:
in the green?

Innocence spreads the smiles of boy and girl
as they search high and low for a spot of blue
wishing to find in that glorious green,
that shining viridian splendor,
that artificial semblance of nature.
Yet near the gleaming azure pickup
bulging with its equipment gifted by mommy and daddy
to that blond boy and girl
who innocently search for that spot of blue
within the chartreuse expanse,
there is another truck,
beat up, rusted, brown or red or dirty conch
with equipment falling out its sides:
vacuum cleaners, tires, metal boxes to fix
every handyman's troubles.

The brown-headed couple divide and conquer.
The olive-skinned female shoulders the vacuum,
her long shining braid glistening in the sun.
She trudges up the grand entryway of an imposing mansion
next to the green.
The swarthy, bronzed man departs,
leaving his partner at the door of this dynasty,
her vacuum cleaner upright
as he heads to the golf course
to begin his work in the rising heat.

Weary even before the start of day
the woman rings the doorbell, ready for labor.
Next to the manicured golf club,
Next to the rolling hills brandished in turquoise,
next to the hole-in-one, she smiles sadly
at the white woman opening the door to let her in.
Already inside the clipped and pared golf club,
looking beyond the gentle slopes wielding in sage
next to the hole-in-one, the man scoffs bleakly
at the teal expanse his lawn mower must travel today.

All the while the two bleached blond heads
beam at each other, at the splendor of a beautiful day,
at the unnatural beauty of their gargantuan golf dream,
at the perfect presents their mommy and daddy bequeathed
them,
today –
their erect and shiny fishing poles –
a bit misfit in that sea of green.

FRIENDS
by Ana M. Fores Tamayo

Friends, whimsy of time slipping by
not grasping its fading flight.
Cafecito sipped slowly while we chatter,
laughing at the girl & boy in that telenovela
we missed during yesterday's 30-minute session
while we gossiped endlessly…
Can't recall the soap opera's name
yet I remember the delicious secrets we discussed
while watching all that nonsense:
our children's angst and joys,
our woes at getting so much work done against the grain—
orals taken, PhD drafts finalized,
recommendation letters always pending.
We thought we were indestructible, you and I,
our friendship would outlast it all—
absent husbands and Disney World and whining kids,
swimming pools and sandy beaches with doctoral theses
and comprehensives sinking our deliberations…

I see a passing Facebook reference to one exquisite child,
a woman now: I cannot distinguish one daughter from the
other. Do you have the same trouble with mine?
Was I that good a friend if I cannot recognize your children all
grown up? One husband divorced, school completed, job
evaporated, country ousted. New life underway: me not in it.
Life goes on. You went to another post. I left too.
Who were we to say that life would hold us close?
Or did all those grad school years belie my dream of
friendship?

I got your Christmas card today wishing me a Merry Merry.

Picture perfect card with all the trimmings of a life fulfilled:
grandchildren now, striking family, stunning home by a lovely
lake. New husband, not the one you fancied in our youthful
innocence. But our dreams, our ideals?
Long ago we were the best of friends; yet now?
When I drink my cafecito I often think of you,
and that telenovela we never finished.

MATRIMONY
by Ana M. Fores Tamayo

Meandering annals traipsing rings in measures of nonsensical
yesterdays at last, we realize too late the passage of time:
thirty-seven years of happiness and pain and love within
existence rambling through the years fumbling along,
acquiring experience including our bounty, our existential
plight, our joy in being, mooning over our love our children
our pain our physical angst only to realize, laughingly, what we
knew the minute we met, that nothing can replace our love –
not money, not physical goods, not ethereal wants –
you are the only one for me, as I am for you: always in
resilience …

LACE AND NYLON
by Christina Hoag

Rosa bit her lower lip and slid open the top drawer of the dresser. She didn't know why she was trying to be quiet. Mrs. Ellen and her yapping Maltese were out, but the moment seemed to demand silence. Rosa reached into the pile of underwear and plucked a baby pink thong, stretching it between her hands. Did the skimpy bit go in the front or the back? She tossed it back in, unimpressed. A black lacy panty with a little red bow in the front caught her eye. How would that one look on her? Or this gauzy see-through number? It would show everything. What was the point of wearing it? She rubbed a shimmering satin pair against her cheek – so smooth.

"Rosa! Rosaaa!"

She startled and shoved the satin panty into the pocket of her apron. She caught the guilty look on her face in the mirror above the dresser and paused. She had nothing to feel guilty about because she had nothing. *They* were the ones who should feel guilty. She pushed the drawer closed and hurried out of the bedroom to the landing.

"I am here, Mrs. Ellen," she called.

Mrs. Ellen's freshly blonded head appeared at the foot of the staircase. "There you are. I need help with ..." She halted. "Oops, sorry. Bags - car." Her mouth went into slow motion. She pointed to the garage.

Rosa nodded. She got it the first time. "Okay, I come."

Rosa trotted down the stairs and into the garage. The back of the Mercedes SUV was crammed with grocery bags. She started ferrying them into the kitchen, immaculate with her morning's work. She had polished the stainless-steel fridge

40

doors and the rack of copper pots and pans to a gleam, the chrome faucets and granite countertop to a spotless gloss. At least it lasted a little longer with the kids gone at summer camp.

Mrs. Ellen entered the kitchen with a check in her hand as Rosa put away the groceries. Between the pantry and the fridge, there was enough food to feed her village back in Guatemala for a month. But here, there was only Mrs. Ellen, her husband, and a dog little bigger than a guinea pig in the house, plus herself.

"I'm going out for lunch. The pool man's coming this afternoon." Mrs. Ellen pointed to the pool outside and flapped the check in her hand. "Give-to-pool-man, o-kay?"

"O-kay." Rosa wondered if Mrs. Ellen detected the mimicking tone in her voice. Of course not. Who listened to a maid?

Mrs. Ellen put the check under the phone on the counter and patted the frozen package of tuna steaks Rosa had just taken out of a bag. "Leave these out – din-ner." She pointed to a packet of steak. "Mi-mi." She gathered her purse and keys. "Oh, don't forget." She made a round motion with the palm of her hand. Rosa nodded. Polish the silver. She hadn't forgotten. "Okay, Mrs. Ellen."

Mrs. Ellen was gone in a swish of linen and cloying floral perfume. The garage door buzzed and a minute later clanked closed. Rosa took out a plastic container of black beans and rice and a bowl of tortilla dough from the back of the fridge. Mimi was sitting, tongue lolling, at her porcelain bowl decorated with dancing bones. The color of her tongue matched the pink bow tying her shaggy hair above her eyes. She cocked her head and the rhinestones on her collar glinted. Rosa pursed her lips. Mimi was a dog. She could wait for her steak.

Rosa scooped a handful of dough and started patting it into a tortilla between her palms. The cadence of slaps back and forth against her hands was comforting. She closed her eyes, and she was back in the adobe hut where she was born, fingers of Huehuetenango's mountain mist seeping through the walls.

Almost sweeping the floor of packed earth, her mother's braid swung like a pendulum on her back as she sat on her folded knees stoking the fire and mixing the tortilla *masa*. Then Rosa and her sisters patted out the dough in bleary silence as the axe blows of her father chopping the day's firewood thudded outside. They tossed the tortillas onto the skillet and the smell of cooking corn rose with the pine wood smoke to the hut's rafters.

But here, the smell was ammonia, and the sound was the fridge humming. Rosa warmed up the rice and beans and ate. She threw a piece of tortilla to Mimi, who got up and sniffed it. Then the dog lay down, her head on her paws.

"   *No te preocupes, perrita*, I'll get your blessed steak." Rosa stood and chopped the meat to feed the dog. Wiping her hands on her apron, she brushed the bulge of the filched panties in the pocket. She'd already forgotten about them. She fingered the silky fabric. She'd slip them on, just to see how she would look.

She entered her room off the laundry and slid the white nylon briefs down her legs, smooth and well-muscled from growing up three kilometers from the asphalt highway. Back home, no one wore underwear beneath their long skirts. She had brought a *corte* with her on the trip north, but she'd only worn the long, wide bolt of colorful woven cotton once since she'd arrived in Los Angeles six months ago. She'd fastened it around her waist with a sash and worn with it the *huipil* blouse her mother had embroidered with flowers. She'd put it on for a Sunday afternoon outing with some other Guatemalans, but none of the others had worn their traditional dress and she felt out of place. Luky, her cousin who had gotten her the job with Mrs. Ellen, told her no one wore their *cortes* here. Rosa folded it into a neat square and stowed it in the bottom drawer of her dresser.

She pulled on the satin panties and hiked up her uniform around her waist. Standing on tiptoes, she viewed her bottom half in a mirror above the dresser. Her family had shared just a small rectangle of mirror propped on a shelf in the kitchen, so she'd never studied her physique before or even thought much about it. Her legs looked as tall as a horse's, and her belly lay in a valley between her hip bones. She turned to look at herself from all sides, then swayed her hips in a little dance and giggled. She could hear her mother's tuts of disapproval, like when she caught Rosa walking unchaperoned with a neighbor boy. "You're too much of a rebel," her mother scolded. "You'll never get a husband if you keep that up." But mamá wasn't here. Rosa let her uniform drop back in place and went back into the kitchen, smiling inside herself.

She went into the dining room and gathered the silver pieces designated for cleaning and started applying the polish by the sink. She looked at the small TV on the countertop. She was dying to watch the *novelas*, but Mrs. Ellen didn't want her watching Spanish soaps because, she said, Rosa needed to hear only English. But Mrs. Ellen wasn't here. Rosa turned on the TV and switched it to the Spanish channel. Engrossed in a love scene, she jumped when she heard Mimi barking at the back door. She looked out the window. The pool men were lugging in their vacuum equipment.

One of them was new, but he looked familiar. Big eyes and an angular nose. She knew him from somewhere. She leaned further into the window. It was Enrique, from her old English class. Her stomach fluttered. He had flirted with her after class several times, then Luky got her the job in Beverly Hills, and she hadn't gone back. That was three months ago. He wouldn't remember her. She grabbed the check from under the phone and went outside to give it to Julio, the supervisor. He thanked her and called to the men.

"*Venga conmigo*, Jose. You're doing the next house. Enrique, remember to wipe the tiles around the sides. I'll be back in a while."

Enrique uncoiled the vacuum hose. Rosa watched, feeling the sun penetrate her hair to her scalp as the truck's engine faded down the driveway.

Enrique squinted at her. "Weren't you in the English class at the Latino Community Service Center?"

He remembered her. Rosa's chest felt as if it were

about to burst. "Yes, that was me."

"Rosa, isn't it? But you don't go any more."

She smoothed her apron. "It's too far from here. I go to a class at a church here in Beverly Hills now."

"*Qué lástima.* Well, I better get to work, or I'll be in trouble if Julio gets back, and I'm not done." He flashed her a grin and stripped off his shirt.

"Me, too." Rosa returned to the kitchen.

Standing at the sink, she forgot about the novela and the silver polishing as she watched Enrique. He slid the vacuum pole in the pool, barely breaking the surface of the aqua water, the muscles in his arms like ropes, his bronze back alive in a sheen of sweat. He crouched at the shallow end and dunked his head, then shook his hair, scattering drops of water.

She took the pitcher of iced tea from the fridge and a glass and went outside. "*Toma.* You must be thirsty."

He drained the glass in a single gulp. She refilled it, and he downed half. "One day I'll have my own pool service," he said. "That's why I keep going to English class. Besides, I get to meet pretty girls like you."

She liked his confidence. He raised his glass to his lips and stared at her as he drank. She met his gaze until her eyelids stung and she had to close them.

"I have to finish cleaning the silver," she said.

"I have to finish cleaning the pool."

Something in the way he said the sentence made her laugh, which made him laugh. They laughed until her stomach ached. She hadn't laughed like that for ages, since a Sunday evening *paseo* in the town plaza where clusters of boys strolled clockwise, and the girls walked arm-in-arm counterclockwise. She had made a face at a boy she considered ugly, and her friends had erupted into giggles.

Her laughter subsiding into ragged breaths, Rosa went back to the kitchen and finished polishing the silver. The garage door buzzed open, and the car pulled in. She waited for

44

Mrs. Ellen to come in, but she didn't.

Then she heard the rumble of voices outside. Then the high pitch of laughter. Rosa stepped quickly to the window and looked out. Mrs. Ellen was standing by the pool with Enrique. He was leaning with both hands on the vacuum pole in the deep end. Mrs. Ellen had her hand on her chest, like she was trying to contain herself. When they had finished the joke, Mrs. Ellen walked towards the back door. Then she turned and said something to Enrique and waved her hand. The rings on her fingers sparkled in the sun. He looked up and smiled. She turned back to continue to the kitchen. Rosa expected him to continue sliding his pole, but he didn't. He stood still, watching Mrs. Ellen walking, as if hypnotized by the sway of her hips. Rosa felt like a hole had been punched clean through her stomach. She stood transfixed, watching him watch Mrs. Ellen, until his head dropped, and the back door opened. Rosa bent her head over the silver. Mrs. Ellen said something she didn't understand and cooed at Mimi who had come running to greet her.

After Mrs. Ellen went upstairs, Rosa heated several tortillas and packaged them in foil. When she heard the truck pull into the driveway, she hurried outside. With parted lips, she pressed the packet into Enrique's hand. He smiled and tugged the ragged end of her ponytail that had landed over the front of her shoulder. Rosa wondered later if he had brushed her breast accidentally or on purpose. It didn't matter. The hole in her middle filled up.

***

The following Tuesday Rosa cheered inwardly when Mrs. Ellen went out on her errands. Today the pool man would come, although Mrs. Ellen hadn't mentioned it. Rosa ironed the clothes in the laundry, her ears tuned to the sound of a vehicle in the driveway. Finally, the expected door slam came, and Mimi barked. Rosa turned off the iron and hung the blouse she was pressing. A minute later the back doorbell chimed. The pool men didn't usually announce their arrival. Maybe it was Enrique.

She opened the door. A bald man with a smile

plastered on his mouth like a Band-Aid stood on the step. Her shoulders slumped. She had forgotten Mimi's grooming session.

"Bow Wow Boutique, here for Mimi." He spoke the same words in the same annoying singsong every time.

Rosa shuffled into the den and scooped up the dog from her miniature four-poster bed in the corner. She handed over Mimi and closed the door too hard. She trudged up the stairs to the master bedroom, coat hangers hooked on a finger and the laundry basket stacked with sheets and towels wedged on the convenient shelf of her hip, just as she'd carried her brothers and sisters when they were small. She put the basket down on the bed and entered the closet.

It was as big as Rosa's room off the laundry, the rails on three sides crammed with clothes, shelves full of shoes, handbags, belts. Rosa pushed apart clothes to stuff in the blouses she'd ironed. A bulky garment bag that she hadn't seen before was taking up a lot of room. She unzipped it. A dark, rich fur burst out. It felt softer than baby flesh. She pulled out a full-length coat. It was surprisingly heavy. She slipped her arms through the sleeves, allowing the coat to swallow her. She modelled herself in front of the mirror on the closet door, reveling in the feel of such luxury.

She pulled off the elastic holding her ponytail and shook out her hair, so it cloaked her shoulders. She grabbed a pair of gold lame high-heel sandals and stepped out of her flat, rubber-soled work shoes. The sandals were too big, but it didn't matter. She liked the line of her calf with her heels raised. She rummaged in a jewelry box on a shelf and found long gold earrings and stuck them in her ears.

Rosa clomped around the bedroom, trying to keep her feet from sliding off the sandals and sashaying her hips. She was mistress of the house now. She sat in a chintz armchair by the window, hands on the arms, and crossed her legs, bouncing the upper one confidently. She imagined Enrique sitting across from her in a fancy restaurant, his hair slicked back, handsome as a telenovela star. Glasses clinked and perspiring waiters scurried like ants at the snap of her fingers. She and Enrique laughed at some unknown joke. She pretended to smoke a cigarette, waving her hand and pursing her lips to exhale. She clutched the collar of her fur and coyly smiled at his advances.

The doorbell startled her reverie. She had lost track of time. She threw off the coat and ran barefoot downstairs to retrieve Mimi, now turned into ball of cotton wool. She deposited the dog in her bed and went back upstairs to put away the sheets and towels along with her daydreams.

When she returned to the kitchen, Mrs. Ellen's purse and keys were on the counter. She heard noises outside and looked out the window. Mrs. Ellen was clapping her hands as Mimi scampered around the yard, then squatted. "Gooood girrrrl!" Mrs. Ellen said. Rosa knew what that meant – she'd have to go out with the plastic bag and pick up the shit.

***

The pool service didn't come the rest of the week. Rosa was resigned. Someone else, it seemed, always pulled the strings of her life.

Saturday morning Mrs. Ellen entered the kitchen in her golf skirt. She took out her checkbook from her purse. "Pool man today," she said as she scribbled out the check and stuck it under the phone. Rosa's heart skipped like a rhythm on a marimba. Somewhere within her, a cord of hope uncoiled.

After Mrs. Ellen left, Rosa shut Mimi in the bathroom and went upstairs to the master bedroom. She selected a pair of red lace-trimmed panties from the top drawer and pulled out a matching bra. She'd have to stuff the cups with tennis balls to make it fit. She tossed it back and shoved the drawer closed so hard the perfume bottles on top rattled, nabbing her attention. She grabbed one and craned her neck to catch the squirts. She went into the bathroom and daubed rouge on her cheeks and mascara on her eyes. She decided she looked like a doll and washed it off. She tried a fuchsia lipstick. That would do. A gold bangle and dangling crystal earrings sat on the counter. She slid the bangle on her wrist. It shone against her dusky skin, then she fastened the earrings in her lobes.

After she changed into the red panties and a clean pink

47

uniform in her room, she looked at herself in the mirror. The earrings sparkled as she cocked her head like Mimi. She smiled.

The truck rumbled into the driveway shortly after noon. She grabbed the check and ran to the back door. Enrique stood on the truck bed unloading the cleaning equipment. He winked at her. She tried to straighten her lips out of their smile as she handed Julio the check.

"I'll stay and do this one, Julio," Enrique called.

"*Está bien*, but don't be long. We've got a lot of houses today."

He got into the truck. The ignition strained to start, but then it kicked in with a cough. The truck lurched off and the yard fell silent again.

Enrique assembled the vacuum by the pool. Rosa went inside and came back out with ice water. Enrique took the glass. "You're the prettiest thing I've seen, well, since I was last here."

Rosa knew he was just flirting, but the words made her swell inside all the same. She waved her hand dismissively. "*Ay, vos*! Anyway, you're late this week."

"The truck broke down, so we're backed up with jobs. I lost two days' pay and now Julio wants us to do more houses in one day for no extra money."

"He should've paid you," Rosa said. "It wasn't your fault the truck broke down."

Enrique shrugged. "Yeah, but that's not how it works. He's super cheap. When I have my own pool service, I'm going to treat the employees real good." He handed her the empty glass. "I better get to work."

Rosa glanced out the window every few minutes as she changed the sheets on the king-sized master bed. When it looked like he was close to finishing, she enclosed Mimi in the downstairs bathroom and took a glass of iced tea outside. He was talking into a cell phone.

"Julio's going to be late," he said as she handed him

the drink. "The truck broke down again. I might be here a while."

Rosa smelled the tang of his sweat glistening on his skin. "Why don't you come into the kitchen, *pues*? It's cooler. No one's home."

"Are you sure?"

She nodded. He hesitated, then followed her in. After he set the glass in the sink, he grabbed her by the waist, pressed her against the counter and planted his lips on hers. When they pulled apart, she stared into his pupils. His boldness propelled her. She tugged his hand. He looked at her with raised eyebrows and a half smile but said nothing. She led him out of the kitchen, up the stairs and along the landing, past the abstract oil paintings that resembled chicken scratches in dusty earth.

"Rosa, what are you doing?" She noted with satisfaction that Enrique's voice had dropped to a whisper, a change from the cocksure tone from a few minutes before. Her power stiffened her resolve. She pushed open the master bedroom door and entered. Enrique stopped in the threshold.

"Rosa, we can't be up here. What are you doing?"

"She's playing golf all day. Don't worry." She pulled him into the room and onto the bed. She kissed him. His mouth resisted, but as she slid her hands under his shirt, he loosened. When she felt him fall into her, she broke away. "*Espera*," she whispered into his ear. He looked up confused.

She got up and went into the closet. She returned with the fur coat and spread it on the bed. She lay back on it and he tumbled on to her. Sunrays made the room glow like butter.

Rosa heard the garage door clank open, and the keys crash on the granite counter, but she didn't move. She heard Mimi's muffled yips and scratches and a high-pitch coo as the bathroom door was opened.

"What were you doing shut in there? Poor baby, poor, poor baby. Rosaaaa!"

Rosa heard the undertone of annoyance in the final

syllable of her name, but she didn't move. She heard the queries and the suspicion in the following silence, but she remained still, feeling the weight of Enrique's head on her breast and the steady warmth of his breath on her skin. Footsteps shuffled up the carpeted stairs. Her heartbeat faster. She was in control now. Her life was her own. Rosa tilted her head toward the doorway and waited.

ROSAS HOTEL
by Diana Elizondo

Founded by
Chuck and
Emelia Franklin,
The hotel glows
with Cajun and
Mexicano flare
as it lures
travelers and
tourists to rest
or call it home.
Saxophones
and guitarras
echo through
the lobby
decorated in
green, yellow
and purple
with Frida's
painting hung
on the wall.

BALCONY
by Diana Elizondo

Looking out
from my hotel
room, I saw
flickers of light
dancing in
the darkness.
a few apartments
and duplexes that
reminded me of the
ones from Reynosa,
while some were armed
with spiked rails like in
Bourbon street.
Tejano and jazz bands
were still heard outside,
even when my slept.

THE FAREWELL DINNER
by Don E. Peavy, Sr.

Jonathan Williams, in response to his mother telling him Kristina was calling, got up from his bed and walked into the kitchen where the only telephone was other than the one in his mother's bedroom.

As he took the first step towards the telephone, Jonathan knew exactly what he wanted to tell Kristina Edwards Collins. He would tell her that it is over between them and not to call him anymore. Then he would hang up the receiver before she could work her magic on him. However, the next step brought him doubt and confusion. His mind said give her up, but his heart pleaded to keep her.

By the time Jonathan reached the telephone, a hot sweat had begun to rush out of the pores of his forehead. He looked at the telephone several minutes before picking up the receiver and speaking.

"I'm, uh, uh, uh, sorry, Kristina. But, but, ah, ah, it's over between us," Jonathan tried to speak forcefully. His voice failed him as did his resolve -- he held on to the receiver instead of hanging it up as he had planned.

"Love is forever," responded Kristina. She ignored Jonathan's remark. "Do you remember telling me that?"

The tone of Kristina's voice, the subtlety of her breathing, and her cool logic unnerved Jonathan. If he was an iceberg before coming to the telephone, he was now a puddle of water. He sat down at the kitchen table and spoke quietly into the receiver.

"Yes, I remember. But that was a long time ago."

"Two years is not a long time when you are in love. Do you still love me?"

"Yes, Kristina, I still love you. That is why I ran over to your mother's house when you called me two weeks ago. I was so relieved when you told me you were getting a divorce. But then your mother let it slip that your husband is stationed at Fort Bliss right here in Texas and comes home on the weekends. I felt like a damn fool."

"Jonathan, I love you and I know that you love me. Love doesn't let go – it finds a way. Love always finds a way to love."

Jonathan became even more confused. The rate of sweat pouring from his forehead increased. He felt nauseated. He rubbed his hand across his forehead and wiped the sweat on his pants leg then bowed his head and held the receiver up to his ear with one hand and with the other covered his forehead as if trying to stop the flood.

"Kristina," Jonathan whispered into the telephone, "when I was in 'Nam I thought about you all the time and wished I could have afforded to go to college to avoid being drafted as you suggested. I thought you would wait for me. I explained to you how much I needed the GI Bill to be able to go to college and be somebody. When I got my sister's letter telling me you got married, I was devastated. I had to go to China Beach for three days to get myself together."

"Jonathan, don't worry, everything will be all right."

"Dammit, Kristina, have you heard anything I've said?" Jonathan sat straight up. His voice was loud and angry.

"Son are you okay?" Jonathan's mother rushed into the kitchen.

"Yes Mom, sorry to disturb you."

"I've told you to leave that girl alone," his mother counseled as she returned to her bedroom.

For a few minutes which seemed much longer, there

was silence. Jonathan remembered from his days as a salesman being taught that when silence appears between a salesman and potential buyer, the first one to speak loses. He remained silent.

"I tell you what," said Kristina breaking the silence. "I'll let you go if you will let me cook your favorite meal. It will be our farewell dinner. That way, we can part as friends, and I can be assured you do not hate me."

"I don't hate you. I could never hate you," said Jonathan. His burdens began to lift as he felt that finally Kristina was listening to him.

"Good, does that mean you will come over for dinner?"

"I guess so. But not at your parents."

"Sure, I understand. My sister is going to the Dunbar High School basketball playoffs in Austin this weekend and I promised to housesit for her. You can come over Friday at five in the evening."

"Five o' clock? Why so early?"

"I don't want to impose on your weekend. Plus, I promised my mom I'd go to the movie with her because dad is also going to Austin."

"Very well, but tell me one thing, why could you not wait for me? I thought we had something special," Jonathan said as his discomfort continued to abate.

"I promise to explain everything Friday. Do you have a pen and paper handy?"

"Hold on a minute."

Jonathan found a pen and paper on top of the refrigerator. He returned to the telephone, wrote down the address, and said goodbye to Kristina then returned to his bedroom where he donned his headphones and listened to Marvin Gaye's "What's Going On?" which was playing on his eight-track player.

Time moved swiftly to the appointed hour. Jonathan turned his 1973 Chevrolet Vega into the driveway of the address Kristina gave him. He gave his appearance a final going over before exiting the vehicle, locking it, and heading for the door. Along the way, he promised himself that he would have dinner and leave, closing the chapter on this part of his life.

"Hi, c'mon in," greeted Kristina, opening the door before Jonathan had a chance to knock.

Jonathan stood motionless as he beheld the beauty that stood before him. This was not the wife child who had greeted him two weeks ago at her parents' home. Instead of looking older and beaten about as she had looked then, she looked much younger than her twenty-one years.

Her hair was back to auburn and was teased into beautiful curls that dangled across her forehead whenever she moved. Her eyes were clear and bright and gleamed with all the radiance of youth at the shore of a maiden voyage. Kristina wore a white evening gown which looked like a wedding dress. She was absolutely beautiful.

"Well, are you coming in?" asked Kristina smiling.

"You look like heaven," complimented Jonathan as he stepped inside the door. He wore a light blue Nehru walking suit he had made while in Vietnam, a black silk shirt, and black patent leather shoes.

Jerry Butler's "For Your Precious Love" came from a nearby stereo eight-track player. Moved by the song and Kristina's beauty, Jonathan fought to steady his course and maintain his resolve.

Kristina, perceiving the tension building up within Jonathan, moved towards him and took hold of his right hand. Unlike two weeks ago when he jerked at the rough touch, Jonathan was invigorated with a surge of power he could not understand. Blood rushed from his heart throughout his body. He sweated; his heart pounded. Instinctively, he pulled Kristina to his body and locked her in his arms, placing his mouth on hers as he fumbled with the buttons of her dress.

"Wait, wait, wait," pleaded Kristina. "Please, let's eat first." She pulled away from Jonathan, closed the door, locked it, then straightened her hair and dress.

Jonathan felt embarrassed that he had lost control so easily – that his shield had been pierced so effortlessly. Still, he was mesmerized by the young woman standing before him.

"Kristina, I know you have spent a lot of time and money preparing dinner. But there is no way I can sit down and eat with you looking so good and me feeling the way I do. It has been over two years and I'm afraid my love Jones has crashed in on me. I want, no I need you now."

Kristina looked at Jonathan and smiled. She wished she could preserve this moment for all time. How she desired to capture this moment like a photograph which she could mount in the scrapbook of her heart where it would remain forever. Sadly, she knew she could do neither.

"Can we at least have some champagne first?" Kristina asked. The smell of the baked lamb chops excited her nostrils. She regretted her plans had gone awry. However, she did not want Jonathan to retreat to where he had been the past two weeks, so she decided to accommodate him.

She led Jonathan into the kitchen and motioned for him to sit down at the table which he did. Kristina turned off the oven, extracted a bottle of Champaign from the refrigerator, returned to the table and poured Jonathan a full glass.

The euphoria of the moment blinded Jonathan to the fact that the bottle was already opened. He forgot the lesson he learned in Germany about always having your drink opened in your presence.

"What about you?" Jonathan asked.

"Yes, but not right now," Kristina answered. She returned the bottle to the refrigerator.

"Here's to love lost and found again. To fires that have died out and been rekindled. Here's to us and the days and nights to come," toasted Jonathan. He raised the glass to eye level then downed the drink in one long gulp. The glass had barely touched the table when Kristina took hold of his hand and led him to the bedroom.

Jonathan's eyes felt heavy. He had expected sleep to come after such a joyous and energy draining experience, but this sleep felt unnatural. Only a faint whisper escaped his lips when he tried to speak. His eyes opened slightly, and he could see Kristina entering the electronics class at high school. Unlike the other girls who enrolled in home economics or cosmetology classes, Kristina was the only girl in the electronics class. Jonathan intervened when the other boys taunted her, and they became friends and then lovers.

Then he saw Kristina at the bus station when he went off to basic training. He got the impression that she was trying to tell him something, but he never could figure out just what it was.

"Sleep my love," said Kristina. She pulled Jonathan towards her and kissed him which replaced his vision with a mist. "And when you awake, we will be in that other world where love is eternal. Sleep my love. I will join you soon."

A bright, encompassing light exploded the mist. Jonathan fell limp in Kristina's arms. She placed him gently against the pillow and kissed him again.

Kristina got up from the bed and gathered their clothes. With care, she folded Jonathan's pants and placed them on a wooden hanger over which she draped his jacket then hung them in her closet. She did the same with his shirt. The remaining clothes she folded neatly, placing them on the closet shelf.

As for her clothes, she took them with her into the bathroom where she showered quickly and dressed. Kristina turned out the light in the bathroom, closed the door, gave Jonathan a quick smile, then went into the kitchen where she washed the glass Jonathan drank from and placed it in the cabinet, following which she made sure all the stove top burners were off. She removed the food and placed it in the refrigerator.

Satisfied that all was in order, Kristina took the bottle of Champagne from the refrigerator and poured some into a glass. She replaced the cork in the bottle which she then returned to the refrigerator. It was her husband's favorite brand. The thought of her husband made her smile as she envisioned him drinking from the bottle before he entered the bedroom as he always did when he came home on the weekend from Fort Bliss. *Men are such creatures of habit,* she thought.

"Here's to us my love. We will soon be together forever. Today shall we meet in paradise."

Kristina raised the glass toward the bedroom door then downed the bubbly liquid, placed the glass on the table, made sure her lips had imprinted on the rim of the glass, then returned to the bedroom. She took a picture of her daughter Joletta, who died at age one from Sickle Cell Anemia, from her nightstand, eased into the bed next to Jonathan, placed his arms around her and hers around him in such a fashion that they both held the picture of Joletta.

Kristina's lips curved into a smile as her mind dimmed with the thought that her husband, who threatened to commit suicide when she told him she was going to divorce him, would not have to live without her as he had feared. She saw Jonathan and her and Joletta in a field of grass under a sky of pastel colors. A bright and encompassing light exploded the vision as she exhaled her last breath.

BORDER TOWN
by Fernando Esteban Flores

The glow of party lights strung out
along the countless cantinas
announce the hour of reverie & camaraderie
Austere places so hard to erase
In the feign cries of the wind
a lost child awakens slumbering shades
A waning bruise on the aching soul
Voices arrive via portrait prints
Grandmother's tumbledown house on Cortez
Sandy unpaved road on the edge of town
A desolate corner wild with
thick Texas scrub & prickly pear
Someone had tied a white stallion or mare
(Doesn't matter now) the world its wide eyes
as it methodically chewed the long, sweet mesquite pods
beneath a candelabra of stars
Petitions obscure border lines
Blessings or warnings drifting like dandelion seed
Darkness enclosing me like Mother's embraces
Listening for her voice to call me home
The light still framed over remote graveled paths
Entering a holy place, a private passing—
To where I stand now—
Understand completely
How some prize privileged lives
while others wrestle for what's left
That it is far easier to be cruel
Harder to be heroic
When Alzheimer's had pressed
Grandmother past the brink
of a trampled reality
she stood at the entrance
of our house rapping at the door
with her cane pleading to be led out
taken back to her little lot on Cortez
asking what time the bus arrived
An intricate film unspooling from her mind
insisting like a child to be taken home

& after taxing trips on foot
through dusty Ciudad Villa Aldama streets
On countless bus transports *al Norte*
in dusty tumbleweed towns
childhood a pair of shoes that never fit
—our unrecorded diaspora—
Settling resettling packing & picking up
You colonized your corner lot
No immigrant in your own land
Held no titles deeds or Spanish grants
like many boast
& worked your plot of earth
until an oasis emerged
oranges lemons limes
The air soaked in citrus
Amá—you outlasted
Grandfather
Your parents
Your first born her mate
an ancestral host
When you were done job complete
after a lifetime of invectives directives
aimed at anyone who ventured far too near
a cold stern *Amos* railing against injustice
urging us toward righteousness
age weakened the grip of your bitter wrath
That great voice of *Woe* quieted
Inconsolable *Consuelo*
You left without last words
Bound to brave a better world
My lifelong tutelary guide
Your life my catechism
Doctrine's devotee
As close to a god
as I would ever be

AMÁ'S MOLCAJETE
(for Consuelo Meza)
by Fernando Esteban Flores

With apothecary fervor
she ground *cominos*
garlic chili pepper
Bits of her aborted dreams
crushed into a seasoning pulp
to please capricious *Chac*
To mitigate our hunger
with the grinding torque
of arms and hands
pounding the ageless rock
round bellied god on three tiny legs
A sacrifice for our survival
Mortar & pestle
Mulcazitl to the Aztec & the Maya
Metates of the pre-Columbian world
Tejolote in hand
I see her now
breaking down
the green vegetal tendrils red tendons
Offerings of her sumptuous garden
like the *chinampas of Tenochtitlan*
Liberating the flavor
of their essential elements
The spirit of the spice
El sabor we would come to love
flowing through her unpretentious kitchen
like an invisible ring
Even the simplest
feasted like kings

Chac—Mayan rain deity; patron of agriculture
Chinampas of Tenochtitlan—floating gardens of Tenochtitlan,
a city-state located in Lake Texcoco in the valley of
Mexico

BLOOD BORN
by Jose R. Castilleja

The moon travels across the night sky,
the blade shines bright,
man hands shock
the friend is no more.
Mayan-Aztec blood runs to the floor.

Mystic sand flies through the moon's floor,
magical being stands tall,
wizards chant rings out,
the son moves no more.
Wizard's blood runs cold.

Mist of the abyss,
deep into the darkness goes,
soul of history,
saving time bright as light,
streams to Earth.

A child is born on Earth.
Good or evil,
the shadow moves now on Earth?

by
Jose R. Castilleja

LA BESTIA*
by Dee Allen

The Southern poor—*La Raza***
Climb & ride on a rather long back
Of a large lumbering beast
Rolling along the iron tracks

Swiftly & steadily, colossal
Heavy metal serpent chugs
Far away from lives in disarray,
Corrupt cops, thugs running drugs

Any life's better than that—
The Beast—sure means of transport
Thoughts cast on money they will make
Working in cities of the North

Honduras, Guatemala, Mexico
Long in rear view—
Most people climb & ride aboard iron skin
Risk mortal danger they'll run into:

Injuries, deaths, deportations
Could happen anywhere
Prices they pay to see a better day
Craving freedom from economic despair

Despite their own hardships, *Patronas****
By the railroad tracks help riders on their way
Bags of food & bottled water hold
Deprivation at bay for each stowaway

May fortune go to migrants, should their feet touch

The domain of dreams immense
Land of star-spangled contradictions
Separated from the South by border fence.

W: 12.19.21
(For Elizabeth Jiménez Montelongo.)
 *SPANISH: "The Beast."
**Spanish-speaking [and by extension, Portuguese-speaking]
Catholic Brown people.
    Literal translation: "The race."
***A group of volunteer women in Veracruz, Mexico, usually
twelve, who give food and assistance to Central American &
Mexican migrants travelling northbound on top of
 export trains leaving from Chiapas.

LA CENA
de Arón Reinhold

Era domingo a las seis y media, el día de Dios, la hora de nuestra cena que ocurre cada fin de semana como la imparable mano del reloj. Padre entró a la casa con un paquete grande en sus manos y con una mirada en su cara de Abrahán. Madre tomó el paquete y fue a preparar la comida sin palabra. Padre se sentó, la silla gimió, y le sonrió al incómodo cuarto.

"Finalmente es el día de Dios." Padre suspiró y el polvo de sus jeans voló como palomas.

"¿Cómo está, padre? ¿Trae mucha comida?" Yo pregunté, aunque sabía su respuesta del paquete.

"Pues, bien. En verdad el trabajo me cansa, sí, pero estoy bien."

"¿Y la comida?"

"Traigo más comida de la que puedes comer, mija."

"¿Cómo conseguiste la carne?"

"¡Ay Dios, fue muy difícil! Fui al corral y traté de capturar un animal fuerte y joven, pues, era como la bestia creía que tenía derechos, jajaja." Padre vio mi mueca. "Pero Dios no les regaló derechos porque tienen un lugar muy importante en su plan. Necesitamos comer, y Dios necesita sacrificios. Es un intercambio sagrado. Hablando de.."

Padre se levantó y fue al altar hecho de huesos tan viejos como este país. Él empezó a encender las candelas negras, y la cera sangraba roja por los lados. Volvió y me miró con una mirada severa.

"Y mija, ¿cómo van tus estudios?"

"¡Preparen sus trajes!" Madre dijo desde la cocina sobre el ruido de cortando.

Padre y yo salimos del comedor para nuestros respectivos cuartos. Mi traje era gris con una corbata con color parecido a una lengua. En verdad, no me gustaba vestir en traje, pero Dios lo requería en el proceso de su adoración.

"Mija, ayuda tu hermanito." Madre dijo, todavía en la cocina, mientras las ollas chillaron.

Mi hermano estaba durmiendo en su cuarto azul pintado con nubes de ensueño. Lo desperté y ayudé con su ropa.

"Hermana, ¿qué hacemos?" Preguntó, bostezando.

"Estamos adorando a Dios, es su día, ¿recuerdas?"

Abrazó mi pierna y me pregunto, "¿Cuál tipo de carne comemos?"

Acaricié su cabeza y dije, "La carne normal, tontito. ¿Por qué me preguntas?"

"Porque no me gustan esos animales."

"¿Y por qué no te gustan?"

"Porque sus ojos me recuerdan a nosotros."

"Ay, pelón! Son solamente bestias, viven al otro lado del corral."

"Pero, ¿si sueñan como yo?"

"Sin importar, no podríamos existir sin ellos. Cálmate, porfiz."

Lo tomé de su mano y nos fuimos al comedor. Podía oler la carne chisporroteando y mi estómago rugió fuertemente. Padre sentó mientras Madre puso los platos. El cuarto estaba de rojo oscuro y parpadeando con las candelas.

"Mija, comienza la oración, por favor."

Cerramos nuestros ojos juntos y empecé a hablar lentamente con reverencia por el orden natural.

"Gracias a Dios por la grasa de las candelas, y los animales que comemos. Gracias por mi familia, y el privilegio que tenemos. Gracias por su mano invisible que toca todas nuestras vidas. Amen."

Abrí mis ojos y vi el plato con carne. La cabeza estaba sentada con la boca abierta. Tenía pelo negro y corto, con ojos verdes medios caídos. Me di cuenta que Dios tenía un sentido del humor, los animales parecían casi humanos.

LA HOMA, 2015
by Magaly Garcia

Facing south on Mile 7 is a lengthy street stretching towards the concrete expressway, which could take anyone anywhere if they were not held back by the difficulty of finding well-paying work. There, on the intersection of Mile 7 and La Homa, by a closed gas station, little wooden houses sometimes host Sunday night fiestas for no reason other than to play music and surround themselves with family and friends.

Whether it is 7:00 pm or 11:45 pm, these parties end only when the food and Bud Light runs out. Slabs of marinated fajita, baby back ribs, chicken wings, and onions wrapped in aluminum foil continue to be placed on the grill, the smoke wafting towards the nearby tables where the women and children sit by the ice chests filled with knockoff brands of soda. Coughing and fanning their faces with their hands, they share family gossip and news from both sides of the border.

"Abuelita Socorro just called me to say I should stay the night here. There were some balazos near the house again."

"Another shooting? Do you want to stay over at my house tonight? I can drop you off at the bridge tomorrow."

As they discuss sleeping arrangements for those who dare not cross the border until daylight, the men splutter in buzzed laughter as songs like La Sonora Dinamita's "No Te Metas Con Mi Cucu" and the Spanish cover of Billy Ray Cyrus' "Achy Breaky Heart" play from the large speakers owned by the DJs in the gatherings. Couples and teenagers dance freely on the dry patches of grass molding into dirt

69

where chairs and tables were not set up. Everyone fits together in the dances, ranging from pale European-roots skin on round faces and sweaty dirty blonde bangs to thick dark locks pulled back in a rat tail on those sunburned from years of exposure to the sun cutting lawns, building houses, fixing roofs, and more.

At around one in the morning, when toddlers are napping on the metal folding chairs, teenagers are sleepily complaining about how boring the Valley is with its "brown grass" and "there is nothing here to look at other than that museum in McAllen," and the old, perverted uncle nobody kicks out of events is making up his own bachata moves, the people scatter. Some walk to their houses two streets away despite the lack of sidewalks and stickers in the tall weeds, carrying Tupperware filled with leftover pico de gallo and mashed potatoes, crossing the street to the other side of La Homa, warning their companions and children, "Run. Some pendejos don't have their high beams on. Look both ways and run."

Most of the people drive since there are hardly any stoplights or lampposts to guide them southward to their homes past Miles 5 and 3. To avoid the possible scenario of encountering a mean drunk holding a gun, mothers and fathers carry their kids to their cars and depart, passing Mile 5's still active taquerias serving tacos de trompo and frijoles a la charra. Sometimes the children wake up during the drive, glancing at the large signs announcing specials on sincronizada combos and saying, "Ma, quiero tacos."
To which the moms promise, "I'll make you some mañana."

As these families head home, they pass by dark houses on both sides of the street, most of which are made of wood and are surrounded by junk cars and bushy mezquite, orange, and lemon trees in their yards. The sound of the car motors alarm indoor Chihuahuas, making them bark incessantly and beginning a chain reaction throughout the rest of the neighborhoods, creating a choir of dogs howling at each other and their owners yapping, "¡Cállanse!"

When they reach their homes, the families settle for the

70

night, regretting not having left the parties earlier so they could rest for Monday responsibilities. At sunrise the fathers leave for work, stopping by the Stripes gas station for breakfast tacos before following the highway. The mothers feed their children and drive them to their fenced schools, passing by the random horses tied to trees and grazing by La Homa, the rubble once known as La Kebradita Bar, and Los Compayitos—a popular hot dog place on the edge of the street famous for its fat hot dogs wrapped in bacon and topped with grilled onions and chile.

The smaller children are dropped off at the E.B. Reyna Elementary School standing in front of the expressway, where they are kissed and given the sign of the cross before leaving the car and marching to class. Afterwards, most parents follow the last of La Homa and take off on the highway to drop off relatives or head to jobs they could only find outside of the city, wondering if someday their kids will use it to head away from home as well.

MAYBE I WAS AN APOSTLE
by José Sánchez

Maybe I was an Apostle.
Maybe you were my girl.
Maybe we both went riding around
All over the world.

Every day, my heart feels like breaking.
My temperature rises like mercury.
I've got a black motorcycle.
To ride through the twenty-first century.
I was there at the Crucifixion.
I don't remember what side I was on.
I saw it later that night on television,
On the Consuelo Milagro Telethon.

I had my black motorcycle.
Your hair was all crazy red curls.
We rode through the barrio at sunrise,
Like we was riding to the end of the world.
There's a light at the end of the Barrio
With a sign up in Spanish that reads,
"La entrada es tu quebrada.
No te rajes!
No te olvides donde vives, por please."

I found you that night in the desert.
The city was so far away.
I had my black motorcycle,
And the first thing I heard you say was,
"Maybe I was your girlfriend,
When you were a punk rocking disciple."
Gasoline mixes with bread and wine and blood
When you ride a black motorcycle.

Maybe I was an Apostle.
Maybe you were my girl.
Maybe we both went riding around
All over the world.

72

MIGHTY JUAN
by José Sánchez

Mighty Juan, he's a Mexican,
But he's only one.
(He's only one!)
Mighty Juan, he'll be the very first one to tell you
He's not the one.
(He's not the one!)
He's only one.
One Mexican.
But, when there's work to be done,
They call him Mighty Juan, oh, yeah!
Mighty Juan! Oh yeah!

Mighty Juan, he's a Mexican,
And, he likes to have fun.
(Doesn't wanna get in trouble.)
Mighty Juan when it's all said and done
He's like anyone.
(I don't wanna burst your bubble.)
After all,
He's only one.
One Mexican.
But, when there's work to be done
They call him Mighty Juan oh, yeah!
Mighty Juan! Oh yeah!

I heard about him on the radio.
Indigeno, Chicano, Mexicano
Turns out, he lives right in my barrio.
He's a demographic individuo.
He is Mighty Juan, oh, yeah!
Mighty Juan! Oh yeah!

Mighty Juan, he's got a girlfriend.
They call her Mighty Juana.
(Mighty Juana!)
She's got a way to get him up and keep him going
Even when he don't wanna.
(Even when he don't wanna!)
Get up! Mighty Juan.
There's a whole lot of work to be done.
Before you can have any fun.
It's a good thing you're not just anyone.
You are Mighty Juan, oh yeah!
Mighty Juan! Oh yeah!

PURO WATO VATO
by José Sánchez

Dicen que la "climate change" va cambiar a todo.
Yo no se, pero dicen.

Dicen que el agua va ser como un tesoro.
Yo no se, pero dicen.

Dicen que, alla en Las Vegas,
Te dan la sangre de Cristo en copitas de oro.

Es puro wato vato.
Es puro wato.
Es puro wato vato.

Dicen que a la Becky Sue le gustan los traviesos.
Yo no se, pero dicen.

Dicen que les canta dulce, sangre, piel, y huesos.
Yo no se, pero dicen.

Dicen que veras la gloria por su santa puerta abierta
Si le das uno or tres besos.

Es puro wato vato.
Es puro wato.
Es puro wato vato.

Dicen que el gobierno siempre tiene el poder.
Yo no se, pero dicen.

Dicen que un nuevo dia va amanecer.
Yo no se, pero dicen.

Cuando no tendré problemas.
Como quisiera que seria,
Pero se que no puede ser.

Es puro wato vato.
Es puro wato.
Es puro wato vato.

TALES ACROSS THE RIVER
by Milton Jordan

Listen again, Miguel, to these long
faintly familiar rambling tales too tall
for library shelves, too vague for footnotes,
that disturbed your wandering inattention
only briefly when you heard them before.

I have often ignored your stories
in the midst of nodding siesta smiles
that failed to mask my blue boredom.
Why should this dusty afternoon create
unusual interest in such drab places?

You've traveled through these dirt road towns and heard
these stories you know are imagined,
but today's a colorful Thursday;
even Saltillo might sound interesting;
the river tales, this time, might be true.

SOJOURNERS AMONG US
by Milton Jordan

A delegation from our parish youth group
came calling on Deacon Ruiz seeking
support for a proposal intended
for Sunday's Council and Trustees meeting
to open their recently completed
Youth Center, gym, showers and five classrooms,
as temporary shelter for refugees
living under the bridge eight blocks away.

Babies are staying there, Dolores said,
We have to do something, don't we?
Arturo said all the kids were for it,
but he didn't know about their parents.

Ruiz, twelve years beyond the river himself,
shook his head. I think that's a good idea;
Charities is looking for shelters
but they'll need sponsors to post the bond.

We should ask the Trustees, said Miguel.
Maybe we'll hear some new excuses.

SIGHTING
by Milton Jordan

We had not heard before the sharp *jeet, jeet, jeet*
that caught our attention from the small stand
of trees along the asphalt walking trail
around our senior living apartments
nor seen the surprising, colorful plumage
you spotted on the dull green Live Oak limb
rising a bit above the scrub Cedar,
and after searching your field guides you settled
on the Rio Grande Green Jay, though Petersen
marked its range well to our south and you wondered,
'What's that bird doing this far up the Brazos?'

MORENCI, ARIZONA – 1904
by Guy Prevost

Many in Morenci wondered about the lineage of
Margarita Chacon. Because of her fair skin, some thought she
was criollo, of pure Spanish descent, for indeed she lived in the
Mexican section on the far side of the mine and taught their
children in a makeshift schoolhouse donated by the church.
But others claimed to detect a subtle dark tint to her coloring –
and these things were noticed in the border town - which led to
the more obvious conclusion that she was mestizo, perhaps the
daughter of Sonoran ranchers. Still, Margarita's high
cheekbones and slightly hooked nose suggested a French
background. One rumor claimed her to be the daughter of an
Irish sea captain and a New Orleans Madam, another had her
living for a time with a Cherokee Indian in Las Cruces.
Perhaps her nine-year-old son Joshue (and not Jose as he was
sometimes called), who had lovely bronze skin, was the fruit of
that relationship. No one dared ask her directly and she never
volunteered any information, only fueling speculation,
especially among the wives of the Anglo managers who lived
on the down slope part of the community. They had a lot of
time to gossip about such matters.

But one thing was for sure. Margarita was well respected,
even by the Anglo women, some declaring her a saint. In
addition to her fluency in English and Spanish, and work as a
teacher, she and her husband Miguel were raising Joshue in an
exemplary way. She kept her humble shanty in impeccable
condition and supplemented her income by working two days
a week as a maid in the home of Catherine Townsend, the
wife of the company doctor.

Catherine did not participate in town gossip and was happy

to have Margarita working for her. They enjoyed a cordial but not close relationship. That was until the day that Margarita gave her some startling news. It was early summer.

Dressed in her black smock and white apron, Margarita was polishing the silver in the dining room of the Townsend house. The company had built this impressive Victorian just for the young couple as an inducement to Catherine's husband Jonathan to accept the job in this primitive outpost.

Seated nearby Catherine was addressing blue envelopes with a fine quill pen. She was seven months pregnant, her swollen belly just touching the bottom of the desk. The women could hear the distant clack of the freight cars rattling over the tracks from the copper mine.

"I wanted to ask you," said Catherine. "I'm giving a baby shower in a few weeks, on a Tuesday, and wonder if you could help out?"

"Of course. But I may have to cut back on my hours after that. I have some wonderful news."

Catherine looked up from her writing desk.

"I am going to adopt a child," said Margarita.

"That is wonderful. And how did this come about?"

Margarita smiled broadly. Catherine admired her beauty, even envied it, the jet-black hair, which she wore straight. Though people, especially Jonathan, had told her she was growing more beautiful with each day of her pregnancy. The women were both the same age, 28.

"It is the grace of God," said Margarita, but without a trace of false piety. "That, and the kindness of the Father Mendin, and the Catholic Diocese back in New York City. You know he's our new priest?"

Catherine had only seen the young priest from a distance. She and Jonathan of course attended the Lutheran church in town. She knew Mendin had arrived only some months ago from France, sent by the church to this foreign mission. Some had said that the poor fellow had expected, was even hoping for, the Wild West he read about in books, and had been somewhat disappointed to find Morenci relatively calm. Billy the Kid had in fact been shot to death only five years earlier one hundred miles away. Still, the priest had settled into tending his new flock, primarily Mexican, for they were the only Catholics in town. And as for the pistol he had purchased to join the ranks of warrior priests, western style, well it seemed there was little use for that.

"It's all happening because of Father Mendin and the Church. Back in New York City…they've had a brutal winter. Many poor children were wandering the streets without homes, abandoned by their parents, or simply left on the church steps or even just dumped into trashcans. The Church has taken them in, but the orphanages are overflowing, and the city is no place for a child anyway."

"That is very sad," said Catherine. "But how does it all work?"

"So, there are many children in need… and the Church has somehow raised money to send them out west and put them in good Catholic homes in the country where there is fresh air and clear skies. Father Mendin told me the bishop in Tucson had contacted him to see if there was a place for the children here in Morenci. And it turns out many of my friends and neighbors are also taking in the orphans." Catherine was astonished and pleased.

"And will you be getting a boy or girl?" she asked.

"I want a girl, and so does Joshue…he wants a sister. He's so excited. Her name is Megan, and she is five years old. They don't give you much information. But acccording to Father Mendin, she was left on the doorstep of the Foundling Society with a note from her mother who said she was starving and too poor to feed the child. She hoped God would have mercy and take care of the girl and perhaps someday they would be re-united."

"We are both "expecting" then," said Catherine. "We are like sisters. May I embrace you?" She held out her arms and Margarita came to her.

After work Margarita made the trek up the hill from the Anglo section. She carried a basket of fresh cookies that Catherine had given her. She saw the miners riding the last cars up from the pit, their faces covered in black soot, their boots clod in dirt and mud. They looked tired. She knew the workday had been shortened, due to a new law passed in Phoenix, but this "benefit" had backfired as the company responded by reducing the wages and demanding more carloads of ore per hour. The miners had struck several years ago, a terrible period when tensions had run high. The whole thing ended in disaster when a flash flood washed out their encampment by the mine entrance. The strike concluded in favor of the company. So, the bad feeling continued.

The miners filed off in two directions as they climbed off the cars and headed toward their respective neighborhoods. The Mexicans went south, to the upslope, while the Anglo miners made their way through the dusty main street to the small residential area by the river.

Margarita was glad that Miguel didn't have to go down in the mine. He worked at the smelter three hundred yards from the pit entrance, and though his wages were less than the white workers who did the same job, they were still higher than those of the men in the pits. Each week Miguel sent back half of his income to his mother and father in Baja California. At least that's what he claimed. Margarita wondered whether there was another woman back there, and a child, but she didn't bother him about it. He was good to Joshue, worked hard, and of course, he was very handsome.

Margarita passed the company store and the Cantina where some of the miners were already squandering their wages. But she enjoyed the guitar music filtering out and wondered if Miguel was inside. That was OK with her.

She approached the church, which was a very humble affair: a kind of adobe dome with a cross on top. Father Mendin had done his best to improve the look of the interior, overseeing the installation of a window and hiring a woodworker to carve a crucifix that reflected the passion of Christ's life. He had been shocked by the crudeness of the church at his arrival because it was so Spartan compared to the majestic cathedrals in his home country.

As was her habit Margarita crossed herself and walked inside the church. It was empty. The sunlight slanted in through the window that Mendin had cut out of the south wall, spilling a lovely glow on the new crucifix. She was hoping to see the good father, but he was not there. Instead, she lit two candles, saying a prayer for her upcoming new child and that of Catherine Townsend. She knew the woman had troubles of her own. She had already suffered the loss of two stillborn children.

A young girl came running up to Margarita when she emerged into the bright sunshine.

"Margarita, I can say all the numbers from one to one hundred!"

"Excellent…now let's go to two hundred."

Margarita left the church and turned south into the Mexican section. The dwellings, like hers, had tin roofs and some had timber construction and others were crafted from hand-made adobe bricks. A neighbor, Elena Vargas, waved from her backyard as she collected dried laundry from the clothesline. Chickens squawked nearby, searching for buried seed. Elena was also going to adopt a child. The excitement of this project was spreading like a prairie brushfire. There would be a whole new generation of children to teach, to raise, to bring joy to the entire community. Some couples who had no children of their own were especially eager.

Finally, Margarita turned down a dead-end dirt lane to the little home she occupied with Miguel and Joshue. Miguel had built a porch jutting out from the adobe and made a timber roof over the porch so they could still enjoy it when it rained. He'd waterproofed the roof with used clay tiles, a gift from the company manager who was replacing his old one in the Anglo section.

It was particularly quiet as she approached. Normally Miguel would be home and he and Joshue might be tossing around a ball out front. She looked in the window and saw Father Mendin playing checkers with Joshue. Beside them was Mendin's dog Tiger, who went with him everywhere.

Father Mendin rose as she entered.

"I hope you don't mind."

"Of course not, father, we're honored to have you here."

She noticed his odd French accent. His Spanish was not good, so he preferred conversing in English. He was dressed in his clerical robe, but a cowboy hat was on the nearby table.

"I'd like to speak with you in private, if that's alright," said Mendin.

"Joshue, maybe you can go outside and play with Tiger for a while. Would that be OK?"

"Of course," said Father Mendin, as he handed Joshue a ball, sure to attract the dog's attention.

Joshue smiled, grabbed the ball, and ran out the door. Tiger followed.

Mendin looked on in admiration.

"Such a handsome boy. And smart too."

"He will be a good brother to the girl."

"Yes, I know. He spoke to me about nothing else while thrashing me at checkers. That's what I'm here to talk with you about."

She offered him something to eat but Mendin declined. He was a man of medium height with a weak chin and thin lips.

"As you know it's vital to our project that the parents be good Catholics, abiding in   Christ. That is absolutely essential to the Society in New York." The man seemed nervous, and this alarmed Margarita, but she struggled to seem unruffled. "And certainly, your qualifications in this matter are unquestionable…with everything you do, I only wish that all your neighbors had your faith."

"Yes?" Margarita sat on a wooden bench. "Is there a problem?"

"It's not you, of course, but Miguel. I'd been going through the paperwork, and I never see him in church, and though he declares himself a Catholic, he's never once been a communicant."

"I'll make sure he comes next Sunday, and the Sunday after that."

"Well, there's another thing. Do you have any proof that you and Miguel, are… well, married in the Catholic church? I didn't see a marriage license in your file."

Of course, Margarita had thought of this. In fact, she and Miguel were not husband and wife. They just told people

85

they had been married back in Vera Cruz, before coming to Morenci. She had invented this story three years earlier, hoping no one would recall that she was here six months before Miguel, and in fact had met him here. The Mexicans in the town didn't care much about this kind of thing. Besides, the way they came and went, often working for a year and then returning south of the border, few would even remember these details.

The priest looked at her gravely. Margarita wanted to dish out the usual fib, but to a priest, she was unable to lie. Instead, she was silent.

Mendin rose from the bench and proceeded to the window. A sliver of moon was just rising over the mountain, which had turned dark and foreboding in the afternoon shadow.

"I've been giving the matter a lot of thought. I wouldn't see any problem if you were to be married twice, would you? A reconfirming of your vows, perhaps, would you and Miguel be willing?"

And Margarita saw the work of God's grace once again.

That evening over dinner Catherine shared Margarita's news with her husband Jonathan and a company manager, Waverly, who had been sent out by the mining office in Kansas City.

"She's no relation to Augustin Chacon, I hope," said Waverly as the Townsend's everyday housekeeper served the soup.

"I'm not familiar," said Jonathan.

"Augustin Chacon, a notorious Mexican bandit. He marauded around the border for years, killing whites for the fun of it, and robbing them as an afterthought. The Rangers finally captured him a few years ago and hanged him on the spot."

"Now I remember. The same Rangers came to Morenci during the strike."

"I don't believe in bad blood," said Catherine, "But I doubt Margarita could be related to such a terrible person. She is the embodiment of kindness. And now she has this wonderful news."

86

"I've heard of the orphan trains," said Waverly. "They were originally started by a man named Brace, a Protestant philanthropist back in Chicago. I hear the Catholics were up in arms…because Brace made sure the children went to Protestant homes, while most of these children are Irish or Italian, who are typically Catholic. So, not to be outdone by the dreaded Protestants, the Catholics started the Foundling Organizations of their own. It's not only "good works," but sectarian rivalry that drives all this."

"Well, whoever and whatever, this can only be good for the children, no matter what faith," said Catherine.

"Forgive me. I tend to be skeptical when it comes to religion. I agree. But speaking of children, how far along are you, Catherine?"

"Seven months."

"And are you hoping for a boy or a girl?"

She clasped her husband's hand. "We don't care. Any child would be a blessing."

Later, while Catherine was overseeing matters in the kitchen, Jonathan and Waverly shared a cigar on the veranda. The light was dying as the sky turned from a blazing orange to the deepest crimson.

"You certainly have amazing sunsets out here," said Waverly. "But I'm not sure I could take it year-round."

"We're adapting pretty well. And we are able to go back East once a year on vacations."

"So, you have no regrets about accepting this job? A man of your credentials, Harvard medical school…moving to the sticks."

"I think it wears on Catherine. But when the child comes, it will be fine."

"I wish you the best with that." The two men knew what he meant. Catherine had lost two children already.

"The woman, Chacon, we were talking about earlier. Doesn't she live with Miguel Santana, the smelter?"

"Yes, I think so. Why?"

"No reason, really. He was a real firebrand during the strike. He's lucky to still have his job."

"They had some valid grievances if you ask me. I'm the

one who treated the victims when the number three shaft collapsed last year. And for the company not to pay for medical care or expenses when they had to take time off…"

"Jonathan, always taking the side of the underdog."

"Well, let's agree to disagree."

"OK, but I have one other concern…this orphan plan, these children, coming out here to live. My guess is that they're all white, the offspring of Irish and European immigrants. Do you think it's a good idea that they be adopted by illiterate Mexicans?"

"Well, for one thing, they're not all illiterates. And I'd never given it any thought." Jonathan shrugged, always surprised by the cynicism of Waverly.

On the way back to his cottage that evening Father Mendin congratulated himself on the solution to the problem of Margarita Chacon's marital status. If anyone deserved to adopt a child it was Margarita, and he was convinced that this little girl, Megan, would only be so lucky to have her as a mother. Though he had come to this part of the world for a taste of adventure, which he had read about in the books of Owen Wister and other dime novelists, this scheme for the orphans inspired him and gave special purpose to his ministry. He could see that the Mexicans, for some reason that was not entirely clear to him, were under the thumb of the Anglo community and the company in particular. After all, why would the Mexican worker be paid half that of the Anglo? And the bitterness left by the strike, which had been catastrophic for the miners, had settled into the Mexican neighborhood like a lingering fog for over three years.

But the prospect of the children arriving had lifted the fog, at least that's the way it felt to Father Mendin. He could recognize a buoyant sense of hope in the eyes of the Mexican miners as he went from each little cottage, shanty, cabin, or house to another, doing the appropriate investigation and making sure about the moral and Catholic credentials of the prospective parents. There were twenty families in all who would be adopting, some who already had children (like Margarita) and others who were childless and for whom this was a special blessing. He visited each place three times for follow up visits and each time he noticed how the family had made little improvements in anticipation of the new arrivals. Ramon Santiago had built a whole new room on the side of his pine cabin where his new daughter would sleep. Mario Santana had completely cleaned up the weed patch beside his house and was planting sweet potatoes. Christina Mariega was busy sewing a new Sunday suit of blue cotton after learning the approximate height and weight of the young Irish boy who would soon be her son. And of course, whenever he arrived Mendin noticed that the holy water and crucifix were prominently displayed in the prospective homes. Bishop Audin would be glad!

And even at church, Mendin observed a new sense of devotion and spirit. The hymns, which had been translated into Spanish, his congregants now sang with greater volume and enthusiasm. There was a definite twinkle in the eye of Benedetta Morega, who would be receiving twins! And even those who were not going to be new parents seemed to share in the good feeling, bestowing gifts to the prospective families, offering help and support.

Tiger followed behind Mendin, a mongrel mix of God-knows-what that had attached himself to the priest on his arrival. Frankly, and this was sinful feeling Mendin admitted to himself, he preferred purebred dogs, like the Peissy-Nancroix Retriever he had grown up with. But soon he appreciated the dog's company. Tiger was perpetually skinny, no matter how much she ate, and he wondered if she was part greyhound. He knew they raced that breed in cities like Tucson and Phoenix. Tiger was so thin her ribs protruded through her short white coat, which made it appear that she was starving. And indeed, when the dog first scratched on his cabin door, and refused to be shooed away despite his persistent slamming of the door, Mendin finally took her in and fed her profusely. But even then, she never seemed to put on weight. She was white except for a brindle swatch across her eyes and nose, which looked like a domino mask worn at a glamorous masquerade. But there was nothing glamorous about Tiger. She had upright ears that never seemed to point in the same direction. Mendin had grown to love her more than anyone, even God. She'd sleep faithfully by his bed. He sometimes woke in the middle of the night to see one of her ears sticking straight up, twitching mysteriously, as if she was listening to the music of the spheres.

By the time he was back in his cabin night had fallen. The crickets hummed and chirped outside as Mendin fed Tiger some slops he'd collected from the butcher. He wanted to build a fire, because it comforted him, but it was too warm for that. He lit the oil lamps and uncovered the meal that had been left for him by another one of his devoted congregants: tortillas and a chile verde. This was Adriana Vargas. He was filled with a love of his fellow men and women. This was something approaching God's grace, he thought to himself, something he struggled to achieve, feel, or experience, but was never sure, in spite of his herculean efforts at the seminary, if it would ever have granted him.

That notwithstanding, having digested the wonderful meal and walked with Tiger around the church grounds, he returned to the cabin dedicated to a review of the Epistles of Paul. He had made this his project for the summer. Settling into his rocking chair on the porch, he placed the oil lantern nearby and put on his spectacles. But then he succumbed to another temptation. He rose from the chair, went inside, and from a bookshelf removed The Adventures of the Colorado Kid by Owen Wister.

Two months later Catherine's friend Miranda had asked her to go with her to the station to meet the train. She, Miranda, was taking delivery of an automobile, an anniversary present that her husband, the company manager, had bought for her from the Panhard and Levassor Motor Company in Detroit. It was scheduled to be on the weekly train from St. Louis. Miranda knew that Catherine was depressed, having just lost her third child during birth, and that she was barely leaving her house for anything at all. Miranda thought this errand might lighten her load and besides she wanted to show off the automobile as soon as possible. She thought they might actually drive it back into town if she could learn how to operate it. Her husband Freelander was busy with something at the mine and couldn't come to the station.

It was a pleasant day for the half-mile walk from the center of town to the station. White billowy clouds gathered to the south, and that usually meant that, given the circle around the moon the previous evening, these clouds would turn to thunderheads by nightfall and there would be a drenching summer rain, a welcome event for this dry season.

The women took their umbrellas, just in case, and in their flounced skirts and wide brimmed hats made their way down the gravel road to the station. Catherine was feeling better. She had shut herself in for two weeks and now it was time to recover. The breeze wafting through the canyon felt good on her skin, warmed by the sunlight. She and Jonathan had not decided on how to proceed from here when it came to children. Better to give some time to think things over. The first thing the women noticed was how relatively deserted the main street was – it seemed people were elsewhere. Well, probably at the station to meet relatives or what not.

As they approached the station, and there was still no train, Catherine saw a crowd had gathered, more than usual for this occasion. And she also saw that the crowd was largely Mexican, and that everyone seemed to be well dressed, in their own brand of south-of-the-border finery. A Mariachi band, which normally played at the Cantina, was poised on the platform. Catherine saw Father Mendin, in his clerical black, at the head of the procession, trailed by his ubiquitous dog Tiger. A big banner spelling out BIENVENEDOS BAMBINOS was draped from the stationhouse roof.

"What on earth is happening?' said Miranda. "What are these wetbacks up to?"

Catherine found the reference ugly but said nothing. She was drawing a blank until she spotted Margarita Chacon in

91

the crowd, dressed today in a beautiful white dress and flanked by her son Joshue and husband Miguel. Joshue carried a bouquet of flowers, like a young man waiting for a woman he was courting.

Catherine hadn't seen Margarita since the loss of her son three weeks ago. She had told her not to bother with the housekeeping for a while. And now it came back to her. Margarita was there to meet her new child, her orphan come from New York. Her little girl.

Catherine swallowed with the pain of this realization. A pain, envy, she had rarely experienced with such intensity. Now the joyful faces of these people seemed to mock her. Catherine was blessed in many ways: she was from a fine Baltimore family; she wanted for nothing and had a handsome and loving husband. She had so much more than these people, but also so much less as she knew she would soon discover. She wished Jonathan were there now, to help her understand what was happening.

"It's the orphan train," she said to Miranda.

"The what?"

"Orphans from back east. The Mexican families are adopting them. Father Mendin put this all together, with the Church."

"Well, that is sweet." And just then they could see the steam pouring out of the stack of the approaching engine. The crowd stirred and the Mariachis began to play.

Miranda barked commands to the workers unloading her automobile from the train car that had arrived minutes before. Catherine loitered nearby, trying to be helpful, and telling Miranda how wonderful the contraption was – she'd never seen anything like it, all metal and silver with pipes and levers and shiny wire wheels. But her attention was drawn to the scene several cars away, where two nuns and a middle-aged man were shaking hands with Father Mendin as the train steamed and hissed. They talked animatedly and then they signaled back to someone, and the children filed off the train.

The orphans were all dressed in blue uniforms and the girls had little white bonnets. One of the nuns told them to keep in line and they obeyed as they lined up near the middle-aged man, who wore a long frock coat. He seemed to be in charge. Catherine was struck by the fresh beauty of the kids, some girls trailing blond locks from under their bonnets, red faced boys from age four to seven, shouting and clamoring even after their long journey, while one of the nuns told them to be quiet.

"My God, they're beautiful," said Miranda who was suddenly behind her. "These are the children you told me about?"

Catherine nodded.

"I had no idea they'd be white, they could be our children, and they're going to be adopted by...this rabble?" She indicated the Mexican contingent.

Catherine was confused. The difference, the contrast, had never occurred to her. But now she saw it of course.

"Look at that one," said Miranda, indicating a lovely blond girl of about five. "She's an angel. And her parents will be these spics, and black Romans to boot. It's an outrage."

"Miss. Broxton, I need you to sign!"

The railroad worker held up a clipboard regarding the automobile.

Miranda ignored him.

"We have to do something about this! We have to get back to town and---"

"Miss Broxton..."

Miranda signed without looking at the document.

"We'll get the automobile later. Come on, let's go." And she started toward town. Catherine didn't move. She was still entranced with the vision of the children, the excited look on the faces of the Mexicans, and Margarita Chacon searching the group trying to figure out which one was Megan.

"Catherine, come on, we've got to go."

Later that evening, it started to rain, just as some had predicted. Inside the cabin of Margarita Chacon her new daughter, Megan O'Connor slept soundly in a newly constructed bed, exhausted by her long journey. Margarita had put the flowers Joshue had given his sister in a vase by the bed. Joshue himself sat nearby, staring with wonder at this amazing creature. Her buttery hair swept across the pillow and her skin was as clear and white as ivory, the light from the crackling fire bathing her in a warm glow. Miguel and Margarita sat by the dining table, letting Joshue have this time with his new relation.

The girl had been confused at first, but then intrigued. The troop of children had walked together to the church where Father Mendin made the final turnovers. Joshue stepped forward first from the new family and handed Megan the flowers. The fresh desert air seemed to invigorate her on the walk home, as many neighbors and well-wishers stood in the front doorways or porches and watched her walk by with Margarita and her family, smiling and showing their delight. "Bienvenida!" some would shout. She liked the flowers Joshue had given her, but even more she reached out and touched his dark skin that made his brilliant blue eyes even brighter.

Presently the girl's eyes flickered open. She seemed disoriented, wondering, and then seeing the flowers and Joshue.

"Hello, Jose," she said.

"Joshue, not Jose," he corrected. "Like Joshua…"

"Joshue" she struggled but said it right. "And the walls came tumbling down!" She giggled.

"Are you hungry?"

The girl nodded. She had been so tired that she drifted off to sleep the moment they entered the cabin. Margarita already had a plate of warm stew ready and invited the girl over to the table. She rubbed her eyes, sat down, smelled the stew. She seemed resistant at first and then took a taste. She took one bite and then began to gobble up the rest.

Margarita again thanked God, fully believing in his grace. The sight of the child eating heartily filled her with satisfaction. Even the hard rain pelting the window, the chill of the outside, didn't bother her. The blackness of the desert sometimes haunted her at night.

But now there was a sudden flare in the blackness. Outside the window, it seemed like firelight, a torch, first one then many parading toward the end of the lane. She heard the sound

94

of men shouting, but could barely make out their distorted figures, like ghosts, through the window. She exchanged a worried glance with Miguel, who got up to take a closer look.

Miguel saw thirty men, armed, carrying torches, rifles, and clubs, and led by the company Security Officer Fenwick. He knew Fenwick from the strike and there was no love between these two men. Miguel turned back to Margarita and Joshue, made a gesture for them not to do anything. He opened the front door and stepped outside.

"Hand over the child," said Fenwick. "All orphans must be returned. You're breaking the law. The others have surrendered their children peaceably and I'm hoping you'll do the same."

"What law?"

"Do you think we're going to stand by while a bunch of Mexican border rats steal these children? Mendin was out of line. This is the Great State of Arizona, and we have our laws. He's being held at the hotel by the sheriff."

Miguel stared hard at the cold eyes of Fenwick. He saw among the posse some of the Anglo men he worked with, as well as the managers of the west mine. He knew what this was about, and he knew there was no use in trying to resist. It would only end in disaster for his family, and probably for the child.

"One minute," he said and went back inside.

Like a female wolf above her cub, Margarita stood over the girl. Joshue understood what was transpiring.

"We've got to give her back," said Miguel.

"No, this was sanctioned by the church. We did everything they asked. And look at this girl. Look what a treasure she is."

"They have armed men. The other children have already been turned over. They will go back to New York."

"That's not where they're going," shouted Margarita, thinking of Catherine. "This is the work of the Anglo women. And they've put the screws on their men. No cojones. They will take the children. They will adopt them for themselves."

"Even so, what can we do?"

"Time!" shouted Fenwick from outside.

"I know these men. They will hurt us any way they can. They are thirty, we are two. They remember the strike and so do I."

Miguel walked to the bed and gathered the girl's

95

belongings: a small green sack with a crucifix, an extra pair of shoes, and a pink stuffed bear. Miguel put the items in the sack, and then brought over the girl's coat and bonnet.

The girl looked up from her stew and seemed to immediately know what this meant. She was used to being obedient, for the nuns, no doubt, ruled with a strict hand. She took one last taste of the stew and then got up.

"No!" Margarita howled, clutching the child to her side. "She is ours now." But she knew it was hopeless.

Miguel gently pried her fingers away from the girl and helped her with the coat. Margarita fled to the other room and wept.

Moments later Joshue stared out the rain dropped window into the swirling firelight of the torches. He saw his would-have-been sister being led away holding the hand of a strange man, carrying a torch. She had taken one of the flowers, which she still clutched in her other hand, and she turned back, waving at Joshue. He waved back as she disappeared into the darkness. He would remember this for the rest of his life.

At eight the next evening Father Mendin looked out from the second floor of the Morenci Hotel to the vigilantes gathering in the street below. In the same room the two nuns, and Swain, the representative of the Foundling organization in the frock coat, waited with the eight children who had not been immediately and summarily adopted by the wives of Anglo managers and workers. This had happened just as Margarita had predicted.

Emboldened by the company support of Fenwick, and the rising tide of their hatred, the crowd of men had a hot tub of tar and feathers at the ready.

"Give us that black Roman son of a bitch."

"Slaver!"

"Child stealer."

"Surrender the rest of the children --- or else."

Mendin found it hard to believe he was the target of these insults. He thought of the revolver back in his cabin and would have retrieved it, given the chance. But he could see this was impossible. And how could this go so wrong? And how could God let it be so?

Now it was a matter of the remaining children. The nuns insisted they were the wards of the church, by the law of New

96

York State, and that the Arizonans had no legal claim to them. They would take them back to New York and sue for their companions later.

The company representative, now holding forth to the nuns, said they were in Arizona territory now, under the law of Arizona, and that he and his men had every right to seize the children to prevent them from being given to non-US citizens, Mexicans, who lived in appalling poverty and filth.

Mendin protested, "I checked every home and while they are not rich, these people are not poor."

"What do you know? You're not from Arizona… you're not even American!"

Outside the vigilantes roared, "Give us the priest!"

There was a knock on the door and the Sheriff entered carrying a rifle.

"I don't like what's happening out there. A territorial judge will arrive tomorrow to decide the matter, but I can't guarantee your safety," he said looking at Mendin. "I only have two deputies."

Mendin again looked outside. He saw the men pass a bundle from man to man toward the cauldron of tar. Then they dipped it in the black muck and rolled it around in a pile of pigeon feathers. It was Tiger. The dog had fled down the stairs in the chaos. Still alive, the poor animal limped away, whimpering, barely able to see through his new coat of feathers. The crowd jeered. Mendin feared she would be trampled to death, even if she survived the tarring.

The men laughed, looking up at the hotel.

"Your dog first, you spic-lover, but we have something more fun for you!" shouted another man as he threw a rope over the high branch of a nearby oak tree. The noose swung back and forth like a pendulum.

Mendin saw Tiger vanish into the crowd. He bolted for the door.

"I would not try that," said the Sheriff, nodding to his deputy.

"No!" cried Mendin.

"I can't let you go. It's for your own good." Mendin struggled but the deputy flung him to the floor. The hotel doors shook with the beating fists of the vigilantes as they called for Mendin's life.

Finally, the Sheriff insisted on escorting Mendin and Swain out of town. It was the only way they would be safe, and it was part of a compromise with the company that they would never return. Mendin refused to leave without his dog but finally he was persuaded. Back in Phoenix the Archbishop suggested another parish, perhaps more
peaceful, in San Francisco. But Mendin had lost his faith, and certainly no longer believed in the grace of God.

A week later Mendin was waiting in the Phoenix station for the eastbound train to St. Louis, the first leg of his long journey home. He was suddenly approached by Dr. Jonathan Townsend who was surprised and delighted by the chance meeting.

"My wife is just on the other side of building, with our luggage. We're headed back east and…what luck. Father Mendin, we've been looking for you."

Dr. Townsend shook his head in amazement. Father Mendin couldn't understand why. He had heard, after he fled, that Dr. Townsend had managed to intercede as the voice of reason during the crisis, having finally argued for the nuns to be allowed to return to New York with the remaining children.

Father Mendin waited and then Townsend and Catherine came around the corner. The woman held a leash at the end of which was Tiger. The dog barked with excitement…Tiger, white and clean with the domino swatch across her eyes! A few scars from his burns but now the embodiment of the Holy Spirit. Catherine let go of the lead and Tiger went running into Mendin's waiting arms.

Mendin accepted the dogs' "kisses" like the highest sacrament. There were tears in his eyes. He turned to the couple in astonishment.

"They came to us that night with a child for Catherine and me," said Dr. Townsend. "But I knew she wouldn't accept her. And neither would I. We were both disgusted by what was happening."

"It was Megan, the girl who was going to be adopted by Margarita Chacon," Catherine added.

"Yes," said Father Mendin. "I heard that you helped… but how… Tiger?"

"The next morning, I heard a scratching on the back door…so insistent," said Catherine. "I found her, on the verge of collapse. At first, I thought she was some kind of wild bird, with the feathers. You can imagine. We cleaned her up. It took days. A lot of turpentine, and baths. She didn't enjoy it I can tell you! And now…well you must take her. This is such luck."

"Perhaps there is a God," said Mendin.

Margarita stayed in the town and treated the newly adopted children of the Anglo parents like her own. Miguel grew tired of the job and even of Margarita. He went back south to his mother – or was it another woman? Margarita was never sure. But men could come and go. Joshue would be different. He would carry the torch for what was right. Margarita drew comfort from this belief. She encouraged him to study hard so he could become a lawyer. Perhaps he would fight in the courts against intolerance and bigotry. Surely God would grant her that.

# # #

The Foundling Society eventually brought suit in the courts of Arizona demanding the return of the children stolen from them by the Anglo citizens of Morenci. The judges ruled that the citizens were right in seizing and keeping the children to protect them from the invidious influence of the Mexicans. The U.S. Supreme Court upheld the decision two years later.

MOURNING MORNING
The Uvalde Shooting of May 24, 2022
by Miryam Bujanda

Tomorrow is another mourning morning.
This one for Lexi Rubio,
today was mourning morning
for teacher Mireles.

May 24th seems so far away now
probably because the city is filled with smoke,
suspended in mid-air.

the density of this haze
only increasing with details
of who was where,
The search for keys,
the windows shattered
as the majority of kids
made it out alive;

but in one classroom
the spaghetti is strewn about,
the table draped
with a floor-length tablecloth
where five boys hide,
Miah--laying atop or beside her friend—
already self-smeared with her friend's blood,
The teacher injured
with three shots and laying there,

The classroom
like a spaghetti-and red-sauce
splattered floor,
peppered with brown, black,
and white gaping sandals,
along with a pair
of green Converse sneakers;
and T-shirts, shorts and pants
Shorn like confetti throughout.

No one talks about the storm -
the hurricane that whirled
in this shooter into Uvalde.

no one talks of the moment
before the hurricane lands:
the high-pitch whistle
that the nation here,
we had stopped
hearing it how long ago;
and those in power
never hear it
because they are
in the eye of the storm,
where it is always calm.

Only those out there
who have seen the hurricane
barreling down their way
as they run against
a tsunami WHOOSH
vainly trying
to save their children.

Only those of us
who see the dangerous
Eye of the Storm
will create shelter
from the hurricanes.

HERE
by Miryam Bujanda

Here

> Water abundant flows
> from the front yard acequia,
> Black wrought-iron blooms
> as petals and leaves,
> silhouettes of safety;
> Watermelons root into sand,
> marbled red and blue bowling
> balls await visitors on sparse grass.

Here

> Border-crossing for
> street-corner red enchiladas with potatoes,
> Spanish hymns
> In roof-less and window-less
> places of worship.

Here

> The sun
> sizzles the dawn,
> scorches mid-day,
> sears sunset.

Here

> A tornado whirled,
> uprooting agave and mesquite,
> roiling joy and hope
> into the vortex.

Here

> We were once happy.

by Dan Brook

by Dan Brook

by Dan Brook
by Dan Brook

by Dan Brook

SOY
de Raquel López Suárez

Ser el Viento me gusta,
así me puedo llevar lo que quiera,
lo que se me antoje;
lo que acaricie mis cálidas
y frías partículas.

Como Viento,
puedo secar la lluvia,
absorber sus fluidos,
sí…
y hacerlos míos.

Puedo desnudar los arboles
ver caer sus hojas.
Probar su savia;
venerarla, hasta la última gota.

Y es así…
soy el Viento
que no explica,
ni se esconde,
mucho menos se detiene.
He nacido del misterio,
de la filosofía de Spinoza
en sustancia, de atributos en libertad.

INSACIABLE BOCA
de Raquel López Suárez

Las alas se quedan
en el ruidoso Mar
                    (las alas de los Poetas).
Ellos salen a encontrarlas
a medianoche
vestidos de seda.

Apasionados van
bajo los ojos brillantes
de la conocida boca.

La madre Luna
refresca sus labios
con licores intensos.
Despertando en sus gargantas
el apetito indomable…
                    (se provocan).
Se estremecen
al trasmutar sus alas,
abrazándose a ellas
en la marea palpitante,
rebosante de gemidos salados,
                    (se desfogan).

RING THE BELLS
by Roberto A. Rocha

Ring the bells,
oh, campaneros

ring the bells
and wake the dead
and those who are dead
in spirit and heart

Prepare an altar
set out the yellow marigolds
look at all the white butterflies
come and play, children
be happy and free

Look at all the fruit and sweets
plates full of tamales, bread,
and even bottles of beer
a feast for those who may have believed
that their days of feasting were over
but we never forgot
we never forget

What beautiful wooden horses
all waiting patiently for you to arrive
There are no splinters so do not worry

there is no pain
except for the one that the void causes
the abyss that serves as a constant reminder
that you are gone
gone but not far

only if the wooden horses
stand tall in the fields of yellow marigolds
protecting the tamales, bread, and beer
as the white butterflies dance, giggle,
and play in the golden fields

Just a few more hours
until we are in your presence once again
longing to hold the invisible you
but you are too free for that
for you belong to heaven now
where you are caressed daily
by God

Ring the bells, oh campaneros
for it is almost morning
and morning is when
joy comes

SALVADOR
by Roberto A. Rocha

Her name was Refugio
era la madre
She had 4 daughters
cuatro hijas
de cuatro padres
The girl's names were
Guadalupe, Esperanza, Maria,
and Rosario
asi se llamaban
a la neta
las hijas de Refugio
those were the names of
Refugio's daughters
no te creas de lo contrario
She also had a son
un hijo también
who, if she could have had her way,
she would've named, "sin,"
for she detested men
they were all that was evil
in her world
and the reason her heart
had turned to stone
however, for being appointed
the "devil child,"
he was a good boy
It was his sisters that
became wild
He broke free
from the family's generational curse
He found strength through prayer
and life in the church
He went to school when he could
and kept his nose to the ground
while his sisters became known
for gallivanting all over town

with men who used them like toys
and then grew tired and bored
left them all with children
that they couldn't care for
but their brother
Refugio's devil son
grew to prominence in their town
then, their mayor, he had become
Because he knew the Lord and His Holy word,
he did all he could to help his family
out of the dirt
and through his example of patience and grace
they all found their worth in this world
they all found their place
And this young man's name?
Refugio's devil son?
His name was Salvador
and he was a good boy

UN CONSEJO
de Roberto A. Rocha

Dame tu sacrificio y
rompe esas cadenas
que te tienen preso
y esclavo de la vida
y el amor

Ya no le entregas tus sueños
y tus pasiones a personas
que les importa madre
de tu paz y harmonía espiritual
esa gente que nunca han tenido
un sueño personal o deseo intimo
esa gente que solamente idolatran al trabajo
dinero, y posesiones
Gente que solamente buscan
control de tu vida
personas que se creen
educados y ponen sus experiencias
sobre las tuyas para poder
tenerte fuerte en sus riendas

¡Al infierno con eso!
¡Que se vayan mucho a la chingada!

HOW TO CLEAN A BURNT POT
by Sheree La Puma

A kitchen is a village built on a steep hill. Precariously.
A museum. A coffee shop. A bountiful food dessert.
The fruit. Strawberry. Little fingerprints on the skin.
A warehouse for cheese storage. An agricultural hub
rolled in on chrome wheels. Selfishly abandoned. The
milk has gone bad again. I have tasted enough of the
world to measure myself by the spoonful. Like sugar
spun into strands with its hard exterior, I have become
a delectable web, short & sweet as a chance encounter.
Pregnant with stories of hands, the country they greened.

It was here in the valley that Trump made his final visit
as president, stopping to admire new sections of the
border wall which left some US farmland marooned on
the other side.

Dreams. Moved to a new location. She skips breakfast.
He is used to elbowing his way to the table, empty.
One meal. A bag of rotting fish. Even the dogs are
hungry. Ribs visible through mangey coats. A child's
laughter. After picking onions, she takes him to the *fields*. He
kicks a ball through trash strewn lots. He doesn't care if the
bread is stale. Wind fills canopies over makeshift stalls.
Mold on tomatoes can be sliced off. Her pot is black again.
Burnt beans can be reconstituted with a little water.
Everything good is drawn to the surface. Cinnamon & dried
cloves. A morning scented stock. Half Tears. Half Hope.

ON LOSING MY HUMANITY
by Sheree La Puma

I am a trespasser posing as a savior.
The swallow at my window knows the truth.
There is no wave fierce enough to wash cruelty
off the hands. I walked the beach. Did not turn
my face around to look you in the eye. I searched
for trash, for waste, for a fouling of sand. Angry,
as if I owned the world. I wanted to erase the shadow
of your breath, your tent, your fire. Damn that empty
pan, the blistered feet of children. I knew that you
were cold. I knew that you were hungry yet mocked
the empty line cast deep for fish, as wife, sister, mother,
crouched on obsidian, smiling. How dare you hope
when there is so little to hope for. I called security,
then shut my blinds. I slept you off. In the morning,
you were gone. I called your name: *migratorio.*
You asked my heart to be filled. Shame is an
open container spilling into night.

DEAD-WINGED
by Sibani Sen

Aeneas asks, "what divides the dead?"
The Sybil answers "those denied passage are the helpless
and the grave-less"

some day you will go to the desert
to see birds tending the blanched bones
nesting in clear sockets

these birds migrate at night
where do they go

their sad cries
the miraculous beating of wings
they cease to exist here

each wish is real then
each wish leaves the face of the earth

they store the light that was lost
un-wing it tonight
fill the dark with eyes

I must think of my desire
winged this way

when they seize me
to kill again
you say I chose it.

ICE MISSION: ERASURE
by Sibani Sen

With a workforce numbering approximately 20,000
dear Hope,
deportation officers, special agents, analysts
I am sorry
ICE stands at the forefront of our nation's efforts
because I left
to strengthen border security
you behind
to prevent the illegal movement of people
you know
into, within, and out of the United States
how much
the agency's broad investigative authorities are
I love you
directly related to our country's ongoing efforts to
but I wasn't able to
combat terrorism at home and abroad.
carry you.

WE: THE PASSAGE.
by Sibani Sen

Who does not understand borders?
The real. A star. The earth, your home.
Unwanted where we are. Unwanted where we go.

I am not your enemy I bring the ghosts of peace.
I still the hour where you can redress the crime
Of your apotheosis.

The violence of tomorrow is here.
Of the infinite better future
You have only now.

Bodies lie in barren holes
Dead where they sacrificed
The daub of blood: come, blessings.

LA LLORNA
by Stanley H. Barkan

I

It was in San Miguel de Allende,
where Bebe and I were students in
the Instituto—she studying weaving,
jewelry making, and painting—I
studying poetry and story writing,
Spanish, and journalism, the
summer of 1968, because of my
project for the latter course, to edit a
mimeographed

weekly newsletter called *El Verano*
for the American community, that
La Llorona was introduced to me. A
friend of my wife claimed that La
Llorona had visited her the night
before. She was the wailing woman
of San Miguel, who haunted the
French Park, with her head tucked

underneath her arm. The story was
that La Lorona was the wife of a
Spanish Conquistador, who, while
he was fighting in what became
New Mexico or Texas or California,
she would cuckold him. If she had
children from these *liaisons
dangereuses* that could be his, she
kept them; if not, she cut their heads
off and buried them in the French

II

Park. One day, her husband got
wind of his being a cuckold, one of

118

his compadres made the sign of the
horn on him, and killed her, cut off
her head and buried her in the
French Park, then killed himself for
his family honor. Ever since, it is
purported that La Llorona haunts the
French

Park looking for her murdered
children. So, it was a good feature
for El *Verano* to have a Quija board
session in the apartment of Bebe's
friend across from the French Park.
There were four of us: My wife,
Bebe, who was a complete non-
believer; my wife's girlfriend, who
was a total believer; her boyfriend,
who, like me, I assumed was
agnostic. We tried different pair
combinations, first me with my
wife, then me with the boyfriend,
then Bebe with the boyfriend, and
finally me with my wife's friend,
who claimed she saw La Lorona.
We asked questions but got no
answers.   Then I

III

thought that since we are in Mexico,
maybe the spirits don't speak
English or even Spanish, perhaps
one of the indigenous languages.
And then I thought, maybe the
questions we were asking were too
insignificant for a spirit to bother
with. But since experiencing the
Mummies of

Guanajuato, some days before,
where there were these many
mummified figures lined up along
both sides of a long cavern under
the cemetery in Guanajuato, all of
which were taller than was usual for
inhabitants of that area, as attested
to by the short steps on the Temples
of the Sun and

Moon in Tenochtitlan. They also had
these characteristics in common:
they were all wooden-like and their
mouths were stretched wide, as if
dying in agony. And I wondered,
what if pain continues after death,
and, if mummified, would that be
eternal?

IV

So, I placed my hands over the
planchette with my wife's friend's
opposite doing the same, and
instantaneously the planchette
started to move. So, just to be sure
my wife's friend wasn't doing the
moving, I insisted that both put our
elbows on the table, locking our
arms, and turning our hands
around, so that any movement on
our part would be apparent,
prevented. Well, I nearly got my
wrists broken. Then I asked the
question: "Do people feel pain after
death?" The planchette moved as
follows: First to the letter "A"; then
to the letters "G R E A T   D E A L
H AV E!" The hair on the nape of

my neck bristled. Shaken, my wife
and I quickly left, scurried back to
our motel, the Quinto Loreto, and
huddled together, shivering all night
long till a very cool dawn and, ever
since, I've thought about if I should
be buried or cremated when I die.

V

Years after, telling this story on a
Halloween night to my brother,
Mark, his second wife, Cecilia, and
their children, I was asked to record
it for a Halloween radio program.
So, we did, with Cecilia playing
eerie background flute music.
The WOR radio host, who

included Sybil Leek and Hans
Holzer and some other notables of
the Occult world, introduced me as
the teacher of an Occult program at
LIU's Brooklyn Center, saying,
"Here's a strange story by Stan
Barkan, who swears it is true." And
I told it, and read the poem, "The
Mummies of

Guanajuato" I had written while in
San Miguel which was published in
the local paper, *El Vocero del Norte*,
in Spanish translation. And now, as
I'm getting nenter vi vayter, closer
than farther, at the cusp of 85, with
remembrance, that I prefer being
cremated to being buried.

CROSSINGS
for Bebe in Poland
by Stanley H. Barkan

A hundred years ago
her grandfather
crossed this bridge,
got on a train,
got on a boat,
came to America.

A hundred years later
his granddaughter
got on a plane,
got on a bus,
came to Przemyśl,
crossed this bridge.

A hundred years from now
her grandchildren
will come to this place,
cross this bridge,
seek & find answers
in the mysteries of crossings.

Przemyśl, Poland, July 25, 1998

Statement by photographer Lucia Martinez:

I am a multimedia artist from the Frontera of El Paso, Texas and Cd. Juarez, Chihuahua, Mexico. I am submitting three photographs [opposing two pages] dealing with resistance against gentrification, displacement, and the erasure of historical memory. The three photographs are "Threads," "Memory," and "Toñita." The contentious space is the Barrio Duranguito where the city of El Paso has harasssed and fenced its mostly elderly and Mexican immigrants into leaving the barrio; however, the community along with activist has challenged the city's narrative and actions with art, scholarship and research, and community outreach. Toñita Morales, a community member and activist who has always fought for the wellbeing of her barrio challenges the city elites with the following quote: "ustedes los ricos destruyen pero nosotros creamos (you the rich destroy but we create)."

in School, built in 1891 for the children of the First Ward. Demolished by the City to build a parking garage.
courtesy of El Paso County Historical Society.

NO TRESPASSING

VIOLATORS WILL BE PROSECUTED
CITY OF EL PASO

ENTRADA
PROHIBIDA

by Lucia Martinez

by Lucia Martinez

by Lucia Martinez

by Antonio Eliaz Lopez
Senor con Sombrero ... unapologetically sends message to President Trump he is not welcome in El Paso, Texas, after racist, terrorist massacre @ Walmart 2019. El Paso, Texas (2019) taken at a Frontera Community Protest.

by Antonio Eliaz Lopez
 La Guadalupana ... Community Street Altar @ site of Walmart
racist, terrorist massacre, where 23 Mexican American Elders,
Adults, Children were murdered, 24 injured. El Paso, Texas.
(2019)

by Antonio Eliaz Lopez
 Healing the Frontera ... la Yerbera que cura y sana la Frontera
@ Mercado Cuauhtemoc, Ciudad Juarez, Chih. Mexico (2021)

JOSEFINA
by Antonio Eliaz Lopez

As a guisado simmered,
mientras amasaba,
when her marido wasen't around,
Josefina would light up,
from under the comal

quemaba
yesterday's Tortilla
over a low flame
until it smoked
ahogando cocina
to cover up the smell

Josefina began cooking desde nina
for her six brothers
who expected her cooking, cleaning, washing, ironing

later,
orphaned out
she was tought to cook
by stern monjas
by desipline, routine and a cedar switch
she learned recipes, technique
from older cocineras, madrastras and hungry men

Men loved Her Cooking
Seeing her bellied up to a stove
She cooked Mexican AND Gringo

She gave birth to five children
One she was forced to give away,
One She left behind
With a promise to return,

129

And she did!
Three she raised with men
until everyone left.

After her last husband died
She cracked all her X'mas and Holiday China
in her kitchen trash can
con la fuerza del pasado y un martillo
se pinto las canas
and her lips
lit up from under her comal
and never cooked again.

NESTOR
by Antonio Eliaz Lopez

The last time I saw Nestor
his graduation picture
was pinned
with a fat sewing needle
to the purple velvet robe of el Niño de Atocha
in a candle lit corner
of the Catedral en Cd. Juarez.

De chamaco,
Nestor was all about knuckle balls,
strike outs & home runs,
white camisetas, starched kakis, high top Converse
& morenito machito boys, like him.

De teen
siempre, animales lo seguia.
that desert conejo
that watched from around the fence
as we drank cheap wine
rolled our own cigarettes
as a full moon
moved over Cd. Juarez, El Paso & Our lives.

that venado running thru UTEP campus
that stopped, staired, kinda smiled,
then ran off.

the circling Hawk
as we cycled from Sunset Heights
to downtown queer bars.

that fat mosca
we couldn't get rid of
that drove around with us

all summer
event to event
in the Catering van.

Nestor was the only one of us
to never leave the Frontera
agusto, feliz, cocinando por UTEP y Natalicio
enamorado con La Frontera
he lived for the daily cotoreo of the cocina,
after work, weekend, all night borracheras
dancing bigote a bigote
cachete a cachete
con la Frontera.

It was our mothers, our sisters
That kept us connected

His mother first lit velas
to All the Maria's
prayed dia y noche

we all prayed for Nestor to reappear

After a year of searching morgues & jails & queer cantinas
Nestor's mom
comenso a castigar the Santos on her altar,
bound them up with grey masking tape,
blindfolded them,
put chiquele over their lips & in their ears,
turned them upside down on their heads,
les gritaba bien fayo,
for not returning her Nestor
uno por uno
hid them
in a closet
until only a vela, a flor, a glass of water was all that sat on her
altar.

She finally put Nestor's names on the list,
became part of a mother chain
marchando

brazo en brazo
puente to puente
en busca
de hijos y hijas desaparecidos

Nestor's picture
pinned to her blouse.

SUNDAYS
by Antonio Eliaz Lopez

sun days

I grate cheese, hago salsa, cocino frijol for the week,
Cycle for empanadas
Sip coffee & burn copal
Pick mint for Sun Mint Tea
All before noon.

sun days

my vecinos marinate carne desde temprano
in Magi & Beer, Cevollitas, Oldies y Rancheras
the smell of mesquite, carbon y yerba drifts over the fence
around one
me mandan plato cada domingo
con el hijo flaquito de las orejas estirados.

sun days

Vienen por la vecina
Doña Maria de Jesus by 9
they return her no later than 1
Misa than Luby's

she says her son's a good boy
pero yo no le veo nada de good.

sun days

la familia de la esquina
that inflated Brinca Brinca for neighborhood kids
grilled hot dogs
every Sun Day
ya casi se ven
casi salen

ICE after misa

ICE after school
ICE checkpoints
keeps them enserados, now.

sun days

Tough girls
with outlined lips
painted on cejas
pierced ombligos

text, ignore me, text

as I water the Bouganvilia
remember Lupita de High School
her bothers besitos
back in the day.

sun days

Sister's call

sun days

Me & Domingo
hang like my laundry
until Monday.

OPEN DOORS AND TEARS
by Rod Carlos Rodriguez

Now humid grass is moist today. The border wall is damp, too,
with childish tears. Stephen Miller gives his daily affirmations
in prayerful, blood-soaked hands. Who has forgotten this?
None would remember this. Is this the new theme-park ride?
How many brown kids will fit in the tent? When the cameras
turn away, the talking heads talk of little more than moist
dreams in stocks and 401k's. Here repeats the drills and calls to
pray to united cages of these merry lies. They fly from
mothers', fathers', tias', tios', abuelas' arms, so many arms cut
down, dismembered. Fend off Winter's silver blankets
clumped against the cement floor. Warehouses, old K-Marts,
containers of human shit in full bloom. Soon Spring announces
another year of arms disremembered, jutting through windows,
crevices, doors. But the grass is still moist. The blades divide
their green between asphalt curbs and coyote streets. Sheets of
black and green are steaming amid yesterday's deluge and
tomorrow's manhole, womanhole, person whole and holy.
Pepper spray this talk with salty dancing close, very close that
sweats through clothes and bedsheets and racy confessions. A
murmur, a fervor drafted to close open doors, in walls, in moist
days. Niña is afraid to touch the blade, the grass, all those
fields promised, abuela, tio, Mamá, Papá, they promised.
Miller's prayers go answered, a vengeance against janitors and
abuelos, gone are the speed limits, limits at all. And news
heads, fake eyes blind, mouths stuffed with cotton and whiskey
screams that spray the rain, the moist torrential gully-washers.

Now dry grass engulfs the fire with tomorrow's childish
memories. All those Millers and Mamás break under buses.
Bones bleach under sol's stare. Bare dreams stay moist even if
the river is ablaze. The tears are ablaze, raze these K-Marts,
play in these barren fields. Open these doors. Open her tender,
moist eyes.

BORDERS AND MUSES
by Rod Carlos Rodriguez

Feet planted, toes curl in dirt
between and around, a wide white line
plows the earth, divides one foot
from the other.

Grass undulates, hot breezes caress
among the blades, a sensual dance
by the edge of a glade, drawn whispers
breathe along one side of the border.

Rotted scrub brush, a patchwork next to
outcroppings, ocotillo blossoms blackened
next to crumbling cactus pads, and screaming gusts
blast through the other side of the border.

Arms extended in crucifixion, one hand grasps a gun
pointed at Liberty's temple, Her eyes
squeezed shut, waits for the weapons
bark to splinter bone and grey matter.

The other hand proffers
a branch from the olive grove planted
with Esperanza's brown hands, its leaves fat
with last spring's rain and tomorrow's sunshine.

Transfixed between the border,
Clio passes from the right ear to the left
and back, the words flood
these images, a kaleidoscope enlightened

and drowned at the same time.

Washington Monument in Philadelphia
by Rod Carlos Rodriguez

I AM NOT YOUR CHIHUAHUA
by Tezozomoc © 2022 03 21

Part 1: Street Stray /Perro callejero

I am not Joaquin, Jose, Tiburcio, Elano, or Max Camelo.
Soy tu pinche tlalollinqui (shifts) and rompedorro nightmares.
I am all the latin names the Spaniards did not want. The ugly
ones, found on those "carniceria" yearly calendars with greco-
roman baroque art from Caravaggio;
that mami brought home con las "groserías".

You 'remember? Pendejo. The ones with the saint's names.
When they told you got to celebrate twice a year.
One name, from some pobre progenitor and one to save your
soul. The forgotten saints of the past San Jasmeo, San
Casteabro, San Goloteas de las Campanas.
You 'remember el cura that offered you
un gansito and a coca, San Buto el Grande.

I am not "El Chico temido del vecindario"
Not looking for gaps, ni pinche puentes.
Nor 'Chente trying to "Volver, Volver",
trying to go back to some mythic propaganda.
I am a rabid perro, baboseando in your 'hood.

I am not your trans-border-crossing post-moderno
post-colonialists chavoruco
Soy un pinche "chinga tu madre" bluesman
from the migratory delta of your
tainted abjections with your incarnate desires.
I am Simon Tolomeo
the trickster "pissing boy" of the Northern tribes.

I am el Coyotero, Lupe Lastes.
Mauyandote a Rebeca Gando.
I am not looking for Grounding,
this is my pissing territory, buey.
I am not your dialectical other,
I am in no need of your dialectical behavioral treatment;
Puto, I want to live…
NO SOY TU CHIHUAHUA

de Tezozomoc © 2022 03 21

Parte 1: Perro callejero
No soy Joaquín, José, Tiburcio, Elano o Max Camelo.
Soy tu pinche tlalollinqui (turnos) y pesadillas rompedorro.
Soy todos los nombres latinos que no querían los españoles.
Los feos, que se encuentran en esos calendarios anuales de las
carnicería con arte barroco grecorromano de Caravaggio;
que mami trajo a casa con las "groserías".

¿Tu recuerdas? Pendejo. Los que tienen los nombres de los
santos. Cuando te dijeron que podías celebrar dos veces al
año. Un nombre, de algún pobre progenitor y otro para salvar
tu alma. Los santos olvidados del pasado San Jasmeo, San
Casteabro, San Goloteas de las Campanas.
Te acuerdas del cura que te ofreció
un gansito y una coca, San Buto el Grande.

No soy "El Chico temido del vecindario"
No busco huecos, ni pinche puentes.
Ni 'Chente tratando de "Volver, Volver",
tratando de volver a alguna propaganda mítica.
Soy un perro rabioso, baboseando en tu barrio.

Yo no soy tu
chavoruco transfronterizo posmoderno poscolonialista
Soy un pinche "chinga tu madre" bluesman
del delta migratorio de tus
abyecciones contaminadas con tus deseos encarnados.
Soy Simón Tolomeo,
el embaucador "niño meando" de las tribus del norte.

Soy el Coyotero, Lupe Lastes.
Mauyandote a Rebeca Gando.
No busco aterrizarme,
este es mi territorio me-ando, buey.
No soy tu otro dialéctico,
no necesito tu tratamiento conductual dialéctico;
Puto, quiero vivir…

140

by Tezozomoc

THE BORDER WAS BEAUTIFUL
by Joseph Ross

I used to think
the border was beautiful.

This straight line linking
the Pacific to Arizona,

a pure geometry, resting
quietly at the bottom of

the state I loved, was born in.
I crossed the border

many times, always
in the back seat of my

parents' car, anxious
for the beach at

Ensenada, tacos from
a roadside stand named

Mercedes. We loved
that place. Its uneven

roof, cloth countertop,
a kind woman with

a crescent-moon smile.
But each time we drove

there, I saw more than
I did the trip before.

Over time, I wondered
about the little boys at

the border. They ran
from one car window

to another, selling gum
and cigarettes. They darted
quick, urgent, pleading

with the impatient Americans
to buy, to smile.

We waited in a long
curving arc of cars.

We sat there in the heat,
car exhaust, my dad's

fingers tapping the steering wheel.
He looked anxious too.

But not as anxious as
those boys did.

Now I see the border
is not so beautiful

as it is merciless.
It is not a straight line

at all. It's more like
a seven-year-old boy

sitting on the curb of
the CBX road, tired,

wetting his lips, knowing
he has more candy

and gum to sell before
he can go home.

TRANSFRONTERIZO
by Lee Martinez Soto

I write from a place of nostalgia,
sepia
-colored glasses
tinting the journey from north to south
south to north
back and forth
for so many years.
that I no longer have
a place to call home.

I am
an everlasting commuter,
the ghost of this threshold,
outsider
and denizen,
part of
apart from.

Of this vague memory of
belonging
I am epochs removed from.
Casita linda,
I no longer know you,
much like I no longer know
the pressed together houses of tu
cuadra
those labyrinthian structures of calles
y colonias
gentes
y pandillas
that I used to navigate
without the need for direction
or the ever
-creeping sense of fear.

I have committed to memory
the parts of you I loved
and those I wish I could be rid of.

I know now that those parts are gone:
the places once bustling with life
are now retirement homes
of these childhood
young adulthood
hauntings and memories
that shaped me.

I am stuck in the past
on the south
en el norte
and afraid of crossing
this gargantuan bridge
to the other side
where this place
I have called home
for over a decade lies.

I wonder, how long does it take
for the dust to settle in
for new memories to be made
for this feeling of
estrangement
to be gone
so I can finally feel
like I am home?

TRANSFRONTERIZO
[Spanish Translation]
de Lee Martinez Soto

Escribo desde un lugar de nostalgia,
lentes de color sepia
tiñendo el trayecto de norte a sur
sur a norte
de ida y vuelta
por tantos años
que ya no tengo
un lugar al cual llamar casa.

Soy
un viajero constante,
el fantasma de este umbral,
forastero
y residente,
parte de
aparte de.
De este vago recuerdo de
pertenencia
estoy épocas removido.

Casita linda,
ya no te reconozco,
así como ya no conozco
las casas pegadas
las unas a las otras
de tu cuadra
esas estructuras laberínticas de calles
y colonias
gentes
y pandillas
que solía navegar
sin necesidad de dirección
o la siempre creciente sensación de
miedo.

He memorizado
las partes de ti que amaba

y aquellos recuerdos de los cuales
me gustaría deshacerme.
Ahora sé que esas partes de ti se han
ido:
los lugares una vez llenos de vida
ahora son casas de retiro
de las memorias de la niñez
y adultez
fantasmas y recuerdos
que me vieron crecer.

Estoy atrapado en el pasado
up south
en el norte
y con el miedo a cruzar
este puente gigantesco
al otro lado
donde este lugar
que he llamado casa
por mas de una década se encuentra.

Me pregunto, ¿cuánto tiempo durará
el polvo en asentarse?
¿cuánto tiempo llevará
crear nuevos recuerdos?
¿cuánto tiempo
para que este sentimiento
de extrañeza
se desvanezca?
¿cuánto tiempo
para que finalmente pueda sentirme
como si estuviera en casa?

MY SISTERS' VOICES
by Lee Martinez Soto

The sound of my sisters' voices
echoes through continents;
names unheard of
from areas of a map
no one cares to learn about.

The 3,462 lights taken
treated as
disposable
worthless
invaluable only
when they meet their numbers,
weaponized for political jabs
of one side
to the other side
of the same fucking coin.

My sisters' mothers' voices
resound through every road,
down to every pothole
every poorly lit street,
through deafened neighborhoods
lit up only by
the sound of yet another shooting,
through the 6 feet under
3 feet under
no longer even under
ground
unmarked graves.

While the unnamed men
stay alive
free
their privacies intact,
their lives
unaffected,
encouraged by a system built
by the colonizers' violence

the machismo
racismo
colorismo
clasismo
discafobia
homobia
transfobia
and the weapons back on their hands

My sisters' voices
beg of us
to say their names,
remember more
than just another number
used as a weapon
as we get closer to yet
another election year,
but the 3,462 voices of my sisters
whose light was stifled this last year
will remain unheard
for as long as this system
that profits off their blood
still stands.

MY SISTERS' VOICES
[Spanish Translation]
de Lee Martinez Soto

Las voces de mis hermanas
resuenan a través de continentes;
sus nombres, inauditos
desde las calles que nadie
se preocupa por aprender.

3,462 luces arrebatadas
consideradas
desechables
sin valor
solo invaluables
en su juego de números
utilizados como críticas políticas
de un lado
hacia el otro lado
de la misma
culera
moneda.

Las voces de las madres de mis
hermanas
resuenan por todos los caminos,
por cada bache,
cada calle mal iluminada,
por los barrios ensordecidos
iluminados solo por el sonido de otra
balacera,
a través de 6 pies bajo tierra
3 pies bajo tierra
ya ni siquiera bajo tierra
estas tumbas sin lapidas ni nombre.
Mientras tanto, los hombres sin
nombre
se mantienen vivos,
libres,
su privacidad intacta,
sus vidas

inafectadas,
alentados por un sistema construido
por la violencia de los colonizadores
el machismo
racismo
colorismo
clasismo
discafobia
homofobia
transfobia
y las armas de nuevo en sus manos.
Las voces de mis hermanas
nos suplican
que digamos sus nombres,
que recordemos algo mas
que los números
utilizados como armas
cuanto mas nos acercamos
a otro año electoral,
pero las voces de mis 3,462 hermanas
cuya luz fue sofocada
solo este año pasado
permanecerán sin ser escuchados
sino hasta que este sistema
que lucra con su sangre
se venga abajo.

MIS HERMANOS DEL OTRO LADO
de Vanessa Caraveo

Ser mexicana-americana, y ver en las noticias a mis hermanos del otro lado luchando cada día por una mejor vida para ellos y sus familias, me hace reflexionar sobre las grandes injusticias de la vida. El río en medio, fluyendo entre dos países que solo nos divide en tierra, no en corazón, y que con cada ola furiosa se lleva los sueños de aquellos que están dispuestos a dejarlo todo en el país que conocen, solo por una nueva vida y la oportunidad de realizar sus sueños. Eso se llama valentía y es uno de los sacrificios más grandes conocidos por el ser humano, que no cualquiera haría.

Siento una gran impotencia al ver cómo son tratados a veces por otros de su misma *raza*, que solo por haber nacido en este lado del río se creen más que los inmigrantes, olvidándose de sus raíces y de la mismas injusticias y discriminación que sus propios ascendientes tuvieron que pasar en sus tiempos. El estado de Texas sigue siendo tan antinmigrante, sin importar lo mucho que aportan los inmigrantes en labores que muchos *americanos* flojos no quieren hacer, pero bien que comen de esas frutas y vegetales que se cosechan en el clima insoportable que solo estas personas que tanto detestan tienen la humildad de llevar a cabo estas y otras labores difíciles.

¿Cuándo llegará el día en que las fronteras no estén cegadas o divididas por el lugar donde uno nació o el color de piel que uno tiene? Si el agua que fluye en el rio puede refrescar y puede suplementar la vida y sueños de todos, y esas olas peligrosas que suben y bajan con tanta furia, y que incluso han sido testigos de muchas muertes entre ellos, realmente no conocen de leyes, ni de crueles injusticias ni de discriminación. Son solo los humanos ignorantes los que crean tanta injusticia y discriminación, olvidándose que en esta tierra que todos pisamos y a los ojos de Dios, todos somos iguales y hay que aprender a vivir como tales sin fronteras, que solo dividen corazones y mentes en lugar de unirnos como los hermanos que realmente somos.

A BORDER OF DREAMS
by Vanessa Caraveo

A river flows between two countries I have ties with,
the United States of America and Mexico.
Two countries I love and am proud of,
as one has blessed me with unimaginable and great
opportunities in life. I have seen with my own eyes
how scores of people are willing to risk their life
to have the very same, and how often we take
what we have for granted instead of being truly grateful
for what we've been blessed with, which has allowed us
to live a good life and provide security for our families,
with countless opportunities to turn our dreams into a reality,
that in other lands would have been much more difficult to
achieve. The other country is where my roots come from
and where my great ancestors came from and is rich in
culture, music, delicious food, and much *folklore*,
where I have enjoyed many moments singing
its wonderful *mariachi* and *música ranchera* that enchants
everyone around with much *alegría* that is incomparable.
I am Mexican American and live in a border town,
through my eyes, no divide nor *fronteras* exist
that impede me from cherishing the best of both countries,
and their beautiful cultures and rich experiences they provide
for those who are not blinded by discrimination, and who
share the same dream in their hearts that all humans have,
a secure and peaceful life for themselves and their families.

LA CHICANA
by Vanessa Caraveo

Born and raised in Texas of Mexican descent
I have lived the unique experience of having the best
of both worlds, and to know the value of both worlds,
two countries, two cultures: American and Mexican.
Yet, I am unable to comprehend the great divide there is
between these two peoples and why an enmity has been
formed instead of a union that values all the good that each
possesses. The American way of thinking about building great
structures and their valiance to fight for their country has
created this great country I am proud and immensely blessed
to call home. There is truly pride in every American heart and
I am one of them. Mexico also shares with its people a rich
culture and folklore with an incomparable work ethic that
other countries envy, where no job is too small, and humility
makes these people loved all over the world, wherever they go
as I have seen. I am also proud to be of Mexican descent and
thank my ancestors for all they have done and for blessing me
with the same values that are still appreciated today. I listen to
music from Selena and Britney Spears. I sing *La Cigarra* like
Lola Beltrán and *The San Antonio Rose* like Patsy Cline. I will
enjoy some *tacos de bistec* like the delicious ones that are
relished in *Ciudad de México* and will also enjoy eating a nice
All-American hot dog at a sports game with my family, which
is a classic.
I am proud to be *Chicana* and to have been born and raised
in the incredible Rio Grande Valley border, that has given me
such a valuable life experience that I would not trade for
anything in the world.

RIO BRAVO
de Wendy Lara

Al caminar escuché un chistido
entre los matorrales abro curioso
y te encuetro ahí tan sereno fluyendo,
te contemplo y escucho lo que me quieres decir.
No tienes rostro pero tienes cuerpo
y un corazón fuertemente latiendo,
puedo sentir tu dolor,
te humillan cada vez que te nombran
"el que divide los paises"!
tú no divides las tierras! tú las unes en hermandad!
en paz te contemplo recorriendo tu sendero
y aún no puedo creer que llevando tanta vida en ti,
cargas en tu conciencia tantas muertes,
no llores! yo lo sé, no es tu culpa,
les adviertes, no te queda más remedio
que arrancarlos de tus entrañas
donde quedaron atrapados y cobijarlos en tu regazo
hasta que sus hermanos "los del otro lado"
en lanchas vengan por ellos.
Rio Grande Rio Bravo
impones tu presencia
en las 2 fronteras.

DESDE EL CORAZÓN
de Nely Gonzalez

Desde hace treinta y nueve años decidimos adentrarnos en algo incierto que nos hizo navegar, a veces sin dificultad, otras veces tuvimos que hacerlo con doble esmero.

Si yo fuera hombre me gustaría ser como tú, que desde que empezó nuestra aventura has sido el corazón, la cabeza, los brazos, el ahínco y el alma que no claudica. Tú has sido el esposo, la roca, la casa y eres el trabajo que te has impuesto sin amedrentarte ante nada. Te he visto apostar por nuestro futuro unidos, sin decaer, invirtiendo toda tu energía, en todo este tiempo en el que casi has dejado la vida.

Desde el primer día, nuestras vidas se separaron. Yo me quedé a esperarte y tú te fuiste a buscar un sueño, otra vida en donde tuvimos que acostumbrarnos a tus idas y venidas. Yo con el amor esperanzado y tú en la lejanía siendo fuerte con tu luz en la sonrisa llena de melancolía.

En aquella soledad no imaginable para mí, fuimos dos soledades lejanas que brillamos sin luz algunas veces, pero con los corazones atados. Tú trabajando en Estados Unidos, en los gines de diferentes pueblos: Lyford, Raymonville, Sebastian y hasta el West Texas en donde te pasabas muchos meses del año respirando el polvo o el tamo que despide el algodón, el sorgo y el maíz.

Doce horas parado frente a alguna maquina sin poder moverte solo aplanando algún botón para que saliera la paca de algodón ya terminada.

Como tú dices: viviendo en barracas sin clima o calefacción, trabajando de noche y durmiendo de día. Poco a poco se te fueron quedando los días incrustados en los sueños no realizados. Los hijos te llenaron la vida de alegría, sus sonrisas fueron para ti como gotas de agua clara que te inundaban de esperanzas el alma cada vez que volvías;

una parte de tu vida con nosotros y la otra parte la ibas dejando cada día en algún lugar de ese camino en tu ir y venir.

Tu principal idea, desde el primer día viniendo a Estados Unidos era trabajar, juntar dinero, regresar, y poner un negocio que nos diera para vivir. Ese es el sueño de muchos, pero pasan los años y el pensamiento se desvanece.

Tú, como les pasa a muchos más, te aferras a ese sueño, no lo sueltas, lo traes contigo siempre como tu principal estandarte. Mi orgullo, mi vida eres tú. Jamás te lo digo, pero hoy quiero que lo sepas. Tu vida ha sido muy agitada trabajando horas interminables en ese ir y venir a visitar la familia.

El trabajo de los que inmigran a los Estados Unidos es por temporadas de cuatro, o seis, u ocho semanas. Sobre todo, los que trabajan en las labores sembrando, cosechando y pizcando cebolla, papa, sandía, sorgo, maíz o el algodón. A esta última cosecha es a lo que más te has dedicado tú por los últimos veinticinco años transportando las cosechas del Valle. Hoy tu trabajo es ser trailero, chofer de tu propio tráiler y transportas algodón de un lado a otro. Empezando desde marzo hasta terminar diciembre recorres las carreteras del Valle.

Treinta y nueve años ya dedicados a contribuir a la economía de los Estados Unidos. Al mismo tiempo nosotros como familia nos hemos sustentado con tu trabajo de acá de este lado.

Quiero enfatizar que has dejado tu vida, tu tiempo en este trabajo extenuante.

TIME, MEMORY, AND OBSESSION
by Roosevelt Campbell

I am life and I am memory
I am life as it happens,
As it is lived and is invented
I'm here and I breathe

A clock to record time
A pendulum to move my senses
Memories that passed
Memories that I continue to re-live

Forgotten moments
Once on paper drawn
Reconstructing a life
Using pieces left behind

A fire is burning
To set ablaze the words
Capricious randomness in my brain
To remember something dead

It's an obsession with time
An obsession with the past
The prodigy of the mind
And a coming to an end

Time that passes, time that forgets
Becoming silence and regret
Memory and obsession
I come, I live, and I remain

TIEMPO Y OBSESIÓN
de Roosevelt Campbell

Soy gente, soy vida, soy
memoria
La vida sigue, la vida pasa
He vivido, he inventado
Sigo aquí, sigo respirando

Un reloj el tiempo
Un péndulo mi cabeza
Memorias que no pasan
Y sigo reviviendo

En unas hojas he
plasmado
Tiempos olvidados
Que mi memoria
reconstruye
Con pedazos de pasado

Momentos memorables
Que quisiera ya olvidar
Caprichosos azares de una
vida
Que mi memoria insiste
en recordar

He encendido una
hoguera
Para quemar lo que aun
queda

Se vive y se siente lo
pasado
Mas solo existe el
presente

Es una obsesión con el
tiempo
Una obsesión con el
pasado
El milagro de la mente
Y las sonrisas de la
muerte

Todo acaba, todo hiere
Es ajeno y es silencio
Pasa el tiempo
Pasa lo olvidado

Llego, vivo, permanezco
Acaricio el final
El final que pronto llega
Y que ansioso yo ya
espero

CONTRIBUTOR BIOS

Diana Elizondo is the author of "Smoked Blood and Lavender" and "Yellow Eye Tea." She earned her master's degree in English and Master of Fine Arts degree in Creative Writing from University of Texas Rio Grande Valley. Diana is also a part time English instructor for Texas Southmost College.

Tezozomoc is a Los Angeles Chicano Essayist, Poet and 2009 Oscar Nominated Activist, internationally published and has been published by Floricanto Press, "Gashes!: Poems and Pain from the halls of injustice", a collection of poetry, ISBN-13: 978-1951088040, 9/2019. Featured nationally and internationally across 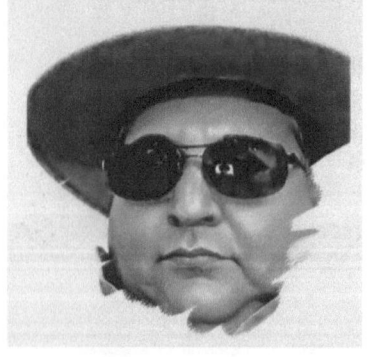 zoom open virtual mics. Published in the following journals /anthologies: 2021 Boundless Anthology, 1/20/2022, MacroMicroCosm, Healing Hands, Vol 7 Issue #3, BC, Canada, 4/15/2021, Rigorous Journal, 9/21/2020, Red Earth Productions & Cultural Work, 12/17/2019, Underwood Press, 9/9/2019, Mom Egg Review, Los Angeles Poets for Justice, 03/15/2021.

Guy Prevost is film/TV writer based in Los Angeles. His background encompasses work as a story editor in Hollywood, college teacher, fiction writer, and *flaneur.* Film credits include award winning episodes of *Walker, Texas Ranger, Dead Man's Gun*, and the SyFy Channel hit *Dinoshark*. His short stories have appeared in *The NonBinary Review*, *The North Atlantic Review*, *Story Quest Magazine*, and elsewhere. He's humbled and honored to be represented in *Beyond Barriers*. More at gbprevost.com.

Born and raised in Edinburg, Texas, **Luke Van Garza** earned degrees in English, Radio-TV-Film, and Cinema-Television from the University of Texas at Austin and the University of Southern California. He worked in script development in the entertainment industry and as

a segment producer for a network TV series. Currently, he teaches screenwriting at Austin Community College. He also serves as a producer, director, and writer of independent films. Luke runs Inner Sanctum Films, the horror division of Starshine Productions LLC, a production company jointly owned by his wife Martha. As of 2022, Inner Sanctum has produced two shorts, SPECTRAL WIND and PETE & RE-PETE; SPECTRAL WIND was an official selection of the South Texas International Film Festival. For more information on Luke and his projects, visit Starshine's official page: https://starshinefilms.com/

Lee Martínez Soto (they/ellx) is a published queer Chicanx poet and translator. Their work centers on mental health stigma: life with comorbid mental health diagnoses, finding accessible resources and competent specialists, and healing. The author self-published their first poetry anthology, Para los Locos in 2020. Additional publications include Chismosa Press vol 4 (2022), Chrysalis Literary Journal (2021), Life in the Time (2021), Chismosas Press vol. 3 (2020), Living Zine vol. 2 (2020), and Nuestras Voces with Massachusetts's College of Liberal Arts (2014). You can keep up with their creative endeavors through their landing page here (https://linktr.ee/cadaveres).

Dee Allen is an African-Italian performance poet based in Oakland, California. Active on creative writing & Spoken Word since the early 1990s. Author of 7 books--*Boneyard, Unwritten Law, Stormwater, Skeletal Black* [all from POOR Press], *Elohi Unitsi* [Conviction 2 Change Publishing] and his 2 newest, *Rusty Gallows* [Vagabond Books] and *Plans* [Nomadic Press]--and 66 anthology appearances under his figurative belt so far. Currently looking for a new publisher to turn his manuscript into a finished, printed 8th book.

Jose R. Castilleja, a writer, a poet, an engineer and community leader. He has written articles of local events, poems for local journals and the local newspaper. He was born and raised in the Rio Grande Valley and has worked in Texas and California.

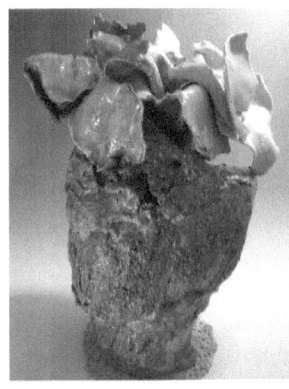

AE Reiff has published *Red Head / A Reparation for Cruelty: Poems of the Unknown Soldier* (Newfoundland Books, 2022), *A Bloody Theory of Divine Light* (2022), *Recon* (Trainwreck Press, 2021), *The True Light That Lights* (Parousia, 2020), and *A Calendar of Poems,* of a mythical history of America. He has writing to appear in the dream issue of *Fiction International*, in *Border Arts: Beyond the Barriers*, and in *Frigg*, a long poem, "Elk and Aspen," where "in a hunter's milieu, a man hacks at some trees with language of a sanctuary against death." He is a native of Philadelphia who has written extensively on the origins of Philadelphia and of the settling of Texas from 1850. He operates a sculpture studio, Forms of the Formless, in the Arizona desert. During business hours he can be reached at Encouragements for Planting. https://encouragementsforsuch.blogspot.com/

Julieta Corpus' poetry has been included in various anthologies, including: *Waiting To Be Heard:Voces desde El Chicho*, *Solamente en San Miguel,Vol. I & II*, *The Thing Itself, Texas Poetry Calendar*, The Valley International Festival Anthology, South Texas  College Interstice, among others. She also collaborated with visual artist Corinne McCormack Whittemore and South Texas poet Katie Hoerth on a book titled, *Borderland Mujeres*, published by Texas A&M Press. Her first poetry collection titled, *Of Love and Departures*, 2021 is available on Amazon. She was recently awarded a Creative Writing Residency in Tasajillo, Texas to translate Austin-based poet, Ire'ne Lara Silva's short story collection "flesh and bone".

 **Milton Jordan** lives with Anne in Georgetown, Texas. He has published poems, stories, and reviews in literary and popular journals for over 50 years. His most recent collection, *A Forest for the Trees,* is out from Backroom Window Press. Milton is editing an anthology from the *Texas Poetry Assignment* for Kallisto Gaia Press.

Ana Fores Tamayo: Being an academic not paid enough for my trouble, I wanted instead to do something that mattered: work with asylum seekers. I advocate for marginalized refugee families from Mexico, Central America, and now, many other countries from which people are being uprooted. Working with asylum seekers is heart wrenching yet satisfying. It is also quite  humbling. My labor has eased my own sense of displacement, being a child refugee, always trying to find home. In parallel, poetry is my escape: I have published in *The Raving Press, Indolent Books, the Laurel Review, Shenandoah,* and many other anthologies and journals, both in the US and internationally, online and in-print. My poetry in translation with its accompanying photography has been featured in art fairs and galleries as well. *Peregrina*, only in Spanish, was just published by *Ediciones Valparaiso* this June 2022.

I hope you like my art; it is a catharsis from the cruelty yet ecstasy of my work. Through it, I keep tilting at windmills.

 **Gerard Sarnat** won San Francisco Poetry's Contest, Poetry in First Place Award, the Dorfman Prize, and has been nominated for handfuls of 2021 and previous Pushcarts/Best of the Net Awards. Gerry's published in Tokyo Poetry Journal, Buddhist Poetry Review, Gargoyle, Main Street Rag, New Delta Review, Northampton Review, New Haven Poetry Institute, Texas Review, Vonnegut Journal, Brooklyn Review, San Francisco Magazine, Monterey Poetry

Review, Los Angeles Review, and New York Times as well
as by Harvard, Stanford, Dartmouth, Penn, Chicago and
Columbia presses. He's authored the collections Homeless
Chronicles (2010), Disputes (2012), 17s (2014), Melting the
Ice King (2016). Gerry's a physician who's built/ staffed
clinics for the marginalized, Stanford professor and
healthcare CEO. Currently he's devoting energy/ resources to
deal with climate justice and serves on Climate Action
Now's board. Gerry's been married since 1969 with three
kids/ six grandsons, and is looking forward to
future granddaughters. gerardsarnat.com

José Sánchez - I grew up in
Weslaco, TX in the 1960s.
When I was 13, I began
writing poetry. Later that
year, I began playing guitar.
Around the time that I began
performing professionally,
at 30, all the poems became
songs. A few years later, I
founded a band, I Ching
Gatos, to perform my songs,
which we still do to this
day.

My college degree from Harvard University is in Folklore
and Mythology A career as an elementary teacher followed,
as well as a Master's Degree in Education from Our Lady of
the Lake University.

Now, I live on South Padre Island. My wife, Lucinda
Wierenga (Sandy Feet) invented Sand Castle Lessons, and so
I am an Sand Castle instructor. With her, I am also an inn-
keeper. We live the artist's life with seven dogs and two cats.
The band plays on.

Rosalva Ruiz, nació en 1981 y es originaria de Weslaco, Texas. Empezó a escribir en 2019 como manera de expresarse. Es miembro de la Sociedad de Poesía de Texas y Códice Colectivo Literario. Algunas de sus obras se han publicado en antologías de Mcallen Public Library, Gnashing Teeth Publishing; también en eZines como Prachya Review, Chachalaca Review, Gnashing Teeth Publishing, Aullidos del Monte (Howls from el Monte) y 52television.com

Rod Carlos Rodriguez has a Master of Fine Arts degree in Creative Writing from the University of Texas at El Paso and has trained as a guest lecturer at the University of Texas at San Antonio Writing Program. He is a poet, fiction, and non-fiction writer who has been writing for over 40 years. He has 3 books of poetry published: the award-winning

Exploits of a Sun Poet (Pecan Grove Press, 2003), *Lucid Affairs* (Sun Arts Press, 2012), and *Native Instincts* (Human Error Publishing, 2016). He is founder/chair of the Sun Poet's Society, South Texas's longest running weekly open-mic poetry reading (1995-2022). He was nominated for the San Antonio Poet Laureate in April 2012, April 2014, April 2016, and April 2018. He was poetry editor for Ocotillo Review, a literary journal/periodical and he was the editor of the Texas Poetry Calendar 2023 (Kallisto Gaia Press).

Joseph Ross is the author of five books of poetry: *Crushed & Crowned* (forthcoming, 2023), *Raising King* (2020), *Ache* (2017), *Gospel of Dust* (2013) and *Meeting Bone Man* (2012). His poems appear in many publications including, *The New York Times Magazine, The Los Angeles Times, Poet Lore, Drumvoices Revue* and the 2022 anthology, *WHERE WE STAND: Poems of Black Resilience.* He has received multiple Pushcart Prize nominations and won the 2012 Pratt Library / *Little Patuxent Review* Poetry Prize for his poem "If Mamie Till Was the Mother of God." Recently, Ross served as judge for the 2021 Ken Ebert Poetry Prize from Iris G. Press. He currently serves on the Poetry Board at the Folger Shakespeare Library in Washington, D.C. where he teaches English and Creative Writing. Ross writes regularly at www.JosephRoss.net.

Don E. Peavy, Sr. is the former editor of a poetry magazine and a former editor of an award-winning newspaper. He has had a book published through a vanity press and has self-published three books. He has had two books published through traditional publishing companies, one of which

became an ethics textbook, so he is in no way new to the writing business. He continues to write while also being the founder and publisher of Prometheus Books, LLC.

Peavy taught religious studies, philosophy, ethics, and administration of justice at the University of Phoenix.

He practiced law in Fort Worth, Texas, before graduating from Brite Divinity School and pursuing a Ph.D. at Claremont Graduate University. Peavy served as pastor of McCarty Memorial Christian Church in Los Angeles and is now a retired minister of the Christian Church (Disciples of Christ).

Arón Reinhold es un Tejano que lee y escribe. Él estudió Literatura Inglesa en la University of North Texas hasta que se graduó en 2014, trabajando subsecuentemente como organizador para efectuar una sociedad sostenible y justa. Recientemente, volvió a la ficción de un amor por el arte y la promesa inherente para visualizar un mundo diferente. Él fue publicado por Wicked Shadow Press y Frontier Tales, y Reinhold tiene próximas publicaciones en Bewildering Stories, Black Petals, Schlock! Webzine, y SavagePlanets. Puede contactarlo a aronreinhold@protonmail.com

Fernando Esteban Flores is a native son of Tejas, a graduate of the University of Texas at Austin, published three books of poetry: *Ragged Borders, Red Accordion Blues, & BloodSongs* available through Hijo del Sol Publishing, published in multiple journals, reviews, newspapers, and online sites, selected in 2018-19 by the Department of Arts & Culture of

the City of San Antonio, with support from Gemini Ink for his poem *Song for America V (Yo Soy San Antonio)* as one of 30 poems/poets to commemorate the City's Tricentennial anniversary, and recently named poetry editor of the *Catch the Next Journal of Ideas & Pedagogy.* Fernando received an ELLA award and an Arts & Letters award from the San Antonio Public Library System and Friends of the San Antonio Library for his outstanding contributions to the artistic and literary community of San Antonio. He is also the founder of an eclectic group of poets, *Voces Cósmicas*, who promote literacy, poetry, and art.

Sheree La Puma is an award-winning writer whose work has appeared in The Penn Review, The Rumpus, Stand Magazine, Redivider, The Maine Review, Rust + Moth, and Catamaran Literary Reader, among others. She earned her MFA in writing from CalArts. Her poetry has been nominated for Best of The Net and three Pushcarts. She has a new chapbook, 'Broken: Do Not Use.' (Main Street Rag Publishing) www.shereelapuma.com, www.twitter.com/shereewrites, www.instagram.com/shereewrites

Antonio Eliaz Lopez is a Cocinero of 35 years, he feeds the Frontera of El Paso, Texas and Ciudad Juarez, Chihuahua. His current writing chronicles the life and testimonies of cociner@s rooted in the Frontera. He is Queer. Chicano. He attended the University of Texas Austin, Center for Mexican American Studies. He is  the founder of Project 7 Serpiente, a border food project.

 **Vanessa Caraveo** is an award-winning bilingual author, published poet, and artist who has a passion for promoting inclusion, empowerment and equality for all, helping others discover the power they possess within themselves to overcome adversity and persevere in life. She is involved with various organizations that assist children and adults with disabilities and enjoys working with nonprofit groups and volunteering in the promotion of literacy. Her work brings focus to many social issues that exist in today's world and has been published in *Literature Today Journal, The Poet Magazine, Latinidad Magazine, Poetrybay, Anacua Literary Arts Review*, and in multiple anthologies throughout the years. Vanessa aspires to continue making a positive difference in many lives through her service to others and literary work.

Christina Hoag is the author of novels *Law of the Jungle, The Blood Room, Girl on the Brink* and *Skin of Tattoos*, and co-authored *Peace in the Hood: Working with Gang Members to End the Violence*. A former journalist for the Miami Herald and Associated Press, she reported from

Latin America for nearly a decade for major media including Time, Business Week, New York Times, Financial Times, and Houston Chronicle among other media. Her short stories and essays have been published in numerous literary reviews, including *Toasted Cheese, Lunch Ticket* and *Shooter*, and have won several awards. Sign up for her newsletter at https://ChristinaHoag.com

Roosevelt V. Campbell is a native of the border region having spent his early years in Reynosa, Tamaulipas and Mission, Texas. His studies took him from the Rio Grande Valley to Baton Rouge, Galveston, Kansas City, and Durham before returning to the area where he now practices medicine. Roosevelt has always enjoyed writing and has written poetry and participated in numerous poetry readings. His work has also appeared in multiple publications and anthologies such as WILD (Writers In Literary Discussion - a student publication at South Texas Community College), diCHo (published by the Latino Writers Collective of Kansas City) and Deranged Perspectives Chapbook and Lost Anthology Series published by the Raving Press.

Dr. Yolanda Chávez Leyva is a Chicana/ fronteriza historian and writer who was born and raised on the border. She is of Rarámuri descent and honors her grandmother Canuta Ruacho. She is the Director of the Institute of Oral History and Associate Professor in the Department of History. She has spent her life listening to and documenting the lives of border  people through research, writing and photography. She is particularly interested in telling the stories of the barrios that grew along the Rio Grande/Rio Bravo in El Paso/ Cd. Juárez during the past 140 years. Professor Leyva specializes in border history and public & oral history. She came to academia after a decade of social work in the Black and Brown communities of east Austin, with a desire to make academia and especially history relevant and useful to people. You can catch her at www.fiercefronteriza.com and IG fierce_fronteriza_fotos

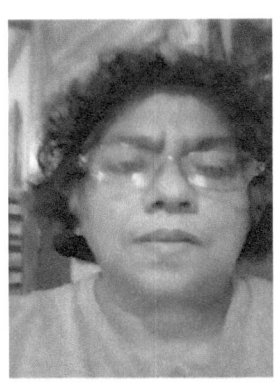 **Lucia Martinez**: I am a Chicana visual artist from the desert and la Frontera of El Paso and Cd. Juarez. I am also a translator and instructor whose works reflect the resilience of border communities. My work has been published by Mujeres De Maiz, and Voces Del Silencio. I collaborated with the poet Jessica Ruizquez and our work was published by the Girl God, Mujeres De Maiz, Sinister Wisdom, and Queers Around the World. I have exhibited my works through the United States and Mexico. Recently I did a workshop for Tumblewords Project and I have a BA in Art and Spanish from the University of Texas at El Paso.

Magaly Garcia lives in south-south Texas and is currently working on a YA hybrid series. She received an MFA in Writing & Publishing from Vermont College of Fine Arts. She has been published in *Running Wild Anthology of Stories Volume 3* (2020), *Fantasy Magazine Issue #63* (2021), *Ink: Queer Sci Fi's Eighth Annual Flash Fiction Contest* (2021), and other works. You can find her on Twitter, Instagram, and Tiktok under the username @ofcatandcacti

Raquel López Suárez. Funda la plataforma literaria independiente Enero Rojo Lunar en 2014 y es editora de la revista digital que lleva el mismo nombre (2021). Autora de *Lluvias acarameladas* (2013) y *Pulverizar la piel* (2021). Editora de *Ámate, salud integral* (2016) y de la antología *Enero Rojo Lunar* (2017). Licenciada en educación por la Universidad Pedagógica Nacional (México, 2006). Desde el 2008 reside en el Valle del Río Grande. Tiene estudios en Teología y Psicoterapia por el Dpto. de Educación y Religión (Texas, 2013). Algunos seminarios adquiridos (2011-2013), con enfoque al desarrollo humano de las universidades: James Madison University (Harrisonburg, VA), Northeastern University (Boston, MA), Universidad de los Andes, (Venezuela), Universidad of Northern Baptist Theological (IL). Participó con su escritura en Festiba, Pasta Poetry and Vino, 100 mil Poetas por el cambio, Voces en la Frontera, Love and Chocolate, Poesía en Atril, Horizonte Sensible, etc. Sus textos se incluyen en *LOST Children of the River*,(The

Raving Press, 2016), y *Revista Literaria* por el Consulado de México en EE. UU.

Roberto A. (Rob) Rocha is a writer, poet, musician, speaker, and podcaster from the Rio Grande Valley in South Texas. In 2014, he released a project of original music titled, "**Dreaming in Blue**," and in 2018, published his first book of bilingual poetry titled, "**Tamarindo Dreams: A Collection of Barrio Poetry**." He has

traveled Latin America, speaking in Mexico, Venezuela, Argentina, and Columbia. In July of 2022, he launched a podcast called, "**The Bridges & Borders Podcast**," which features conversations with notable Latinx, discussing Art, Music, Writing, and Tejano culture. Some of his latest poetry is available in online publications and will be included in an upcoming Texas anthology. Roberto's official FB page is: www.facebook.com/merogallowritings. Contact Roberto for speaking engagements and/or poetry readings at merogallowritings@gmail.com. He currently resides near Dallas, Texas with his wife, Pauline. They have 4 adult children and are expecting their 10th grandchild.

Stanley H. Barkan, editor/ publisher of Cross-Cultural Communications, which in 2020 celebrated its 50th Anniversary with 500 books in print, and as many broadsides and postcards and audio-visual productions in 60 languages (ranging from Arabic to Yiddish). CCC, in addition to having a long and productive cooperative

Photograph by Mark Polyakov

relationship with Peter Thabit Jones of The Seventh Quarry Press in Swansea, Wales, has also hosted numerous literary events throughout the United States and in many parts of the world (Argentina, Bulgaria, Poland, Puerto Rico, Sicily, Wales), at such locations in New York as the International Center, Poets House, the Yale Club, and the Dag Hammerskjöld Auditorium of the United Nations. His own work has been published in 29 poetry editions, many bilingual, including Armenian, Bulgarian, Chinese, Dutch, Farsi/Persian, Italian, Romanian, Russian, Sicilian, Spanish. His most recent books are *As Still as a Broom*, translated into Spanish by Isaac Goldemberg (2018) and *Pumpernickel*, translated into Farsi/Persian by Sepideh Zamani (2019) (both published by Oyster Bay, NY: New Feral Press), and *More Mishpocheh*, with illustrative photos and art by the author's wife, Bebe Barkan (Swansea, Wales: The Seventh Quarry Press, 2018). Also, in 2017, he was awarded the Homer European Medal of Poetry & Art. Barkan lives with his wife in Merrick, Long Island, where his son and daughter and five grandchildren also reside.
http://en.wikipedia.org/wiki/Stanley H. Barkan

Dan Brook's most recent books are *Harboring Happiness: 101 Ways To Be Happy* (Beacon, 2021), *Sweet Nothings* (Hekate, 2020), about the nature of haiku and the concept of nothing, and *Eating the Earth: The Truth About What We Eat* (Smashwords, 2020).

Wendy Lara es una artista multifacética, reconocida por su desempeño actoral en teatro y televisión; ha participado en cortometrajes, comerciales y obras de teatro como actriz, escritora y directora. Diseñadora y creadora de vestuarios siendo sus creaciones más reconocidas en este rubro los diseños de La Catrina Garbancera y Frida Kahlo. En el mundo de las letras creadora de monólogos y poemas algunos de ellos incluidos en diferentes medios electrónicos y libros físicos. Su desempeño artístico tiene fundamento en el empoderamiento de la mujer mexicana como también la fusión de las diferentes ramas artísticas.

Victor M. Parlatto is a poet, father, and writer. With over a decade of experience, Victor has written countless poems and literary works. Well known for his poems addressed to Bella, Victor's poetry paints a picture of everyday life and the emotional spectrum in a comedic, dark, and occasionally

brutally honest light. Victor attends poetry readings weekly and shares personal readings across his social media platforms alongside his written work. Some of these works include: "***" and "***". When Victor is not immersed in his writing, he spends his time with his daughter, gaming, reading, or listening to music.

Nely González nacio en Mainero tamaulipas. Es escritora de poesía. Actriz de teatro y aficionada a la pintura al oleo. Su primer libro(Un Corazón en Soledad) en 2017 Y el segundo libro (Una Carta y Cien Poemas para ti.) Ambos fueron publicados por Legado Publishing.

Actualmente vive en McAllen Texas. Este tercer libro(Mi Vida Sin Ti) esta dedicado a su esposo fallecido el 5 Enero de 2021 En las primeras paginas se daran cuenta que va relatando su vida y que muchas veces es dentro de la cotidianidad del matrimonio que estan juntos pero viven lejos uno del otro. La segunda parte del libro son historias veridicas.

Sibani Sen's poetry has appeared in a variety of publications including Off the Coast, Nixes Mate Review, and Main Street Rag. She has done collaborative projects with the History Design Studio at the Harvard Hutchins Center, the Concord Museum, the Beacon  Street Arts Studios in Somerville, the former Green Street Studio in Cambridge, and the pop-up New Rasa Initiative group at the Public Theater in NYC. Her current projects include forthcoming poetry and a monograph on the Indian pre-modern poet Bharatchandra. She teaches creative writing and South Asian history and literature.

Amanda Lee Calderon is a photographer, writer, filmmaker, and actress from McAllen, Texas. Her photography and poetry have been featured in Encore Magazine, The Paper, Speechless in the RGV Magazine, Mirrors: An Anthology, House of Horrors, House of Horrors 2, and Otherwise Engaged Volume 3. She has written over 10+ screenplays and enjoys shooting short films during her free time. One of her biggest inspirations is nature and enjoying the outdoors.

Miryam Bujanda is a social justice advocate, particularly of women and marginalized communities. She is the Principal of Bujanda & Associates, a Governmental and Community Relations firm. She adjuncts at St. Mary's University on civic and social engagement and is a

Macondo Writer's Workshop alumna. She is writing a poetry memoir that explores the impact of childhood trauma. Inspired by artist K. Hokusai's thirty-six prints of Mt. Fuji, the poetry records the diverse iterations of the traumatic experience and its aftermath, revealing the emergence of new landscapes, which the poet observes, scrutinizes and interprets across the seasons.

179

Kathleen Bunyan Carlson writes a variety of poetry from serious to humorous, and in a variety of forms from sonnets to doggerel. Her content ranges from earthworms making shameless love on a summer day to the pain of losing a child. Kathleen started writing poetry at the age of seven and made writing her profession. She earned a BA in English, MS in Journalism and an MA in Creative Writing. She worked as a technical writer, grant writer and project coordinator for city and county governments, and for a technical college in Wisconsin. She was born on the island of Aruba, Netherlands Antilles. She and her family immigrated to Wisconsin in 1953. She became a U.S. citizen in 1974. She and her husband Vernon live in Palmview, Texas.

Gabriel H. Sanchez is the founder and editor-in-chief for The Raving Press, an indie publisher in the Rio Grande Valley on the U.S.-Mexico border.

www.ingramcontent.com/pod-product-compliance
Lightning Source LLC
Chambersburg PA
CBHW021231020726
47498CB00008B/2790